THE GOOD PHARMACIST'S DEADLY SECRETS

A FINDALE FAE MYSTERY

BELINDA M GORDON

Cover Design by Wesley Goulart
wgoulartt@gmail.com

Publisher:
Shaggy Dog Productions, LLC
www.shaggydogproductions.online

To my dear friends, the Lady Writers of the Poconos.
Without their loving support this book may not have happened.

NEWSLETTER

Sign up to be on the author's VIP List to be the first
to hear about new releases, specials and contests!
Go to:

www.belinda-gordon.com/newsletter/

*M*ax, my floppy-eared cocker spaniel, stood on his hind legs and scratched excitedly at the trailer door, his blond stump of a tail wagging back and forth behind him—antics meant to remind me that I hadn't let him out for his morning walk—as if I needed another reminder of how late I was running.

I grabbed the FedEx box from my tiny kitchen table with a sigh and rushed to the door. As I reached for the doorknob, I glanced longingly at the cold coffeemaker on the counter. Time was not on my side and my longing for my morning fix of the hot brew would have to wait until we reached the café.

I had only opened the door a slight few inches when Max squeezed past me and made a mad dash down the metal steps. He ran, zigzagging across the yard in front of the trailer with his nose to the ground.

"Hurry up, Max," I said, walking to my car. If I didn't push him along, he would spend the whole day investigating the scents left by the animals that had scurried past during the night.

Preoccupied, I almost dropped the box on the hood of my burgundy '68 Ford Mustang. I managed to stop myself in time to avoid scratching the newly refurbished paint job, laying it on the ground instead before digging into my jeans pocket for my keys.

I jerked my head around as a sudden movement caught my attention from the corner of my eye. Two squirrels chased each other down a tree and darted across Max's path. I cursed under my breath, anticipating his reaction.

Several high-pitched barks later and the chase was on.

"Max, HEEL!" I shouted with no real hope my words would penetrate his thick skull. Frustrated, I continued yelling as if he could understand my words. "Mrs. Krauss will freak if we don't get to the café soon."

I ran after him, dreading the chewing out in store for me from the café's proprietor when I didn't keep my promise to fix her dishwasher before the morning rush. It had been bad enough when I told her I had to order a part to complete the repair.

The cocker spaniel sprinted too fast for me to catch him, but I wanted to stay close enough to regain control when the squirrels inevitably lost him.

The squirrels dashed across the dilapidated road in front of the trailer with Max close behind. I reached the near side of the road just in time to see them scurry up a tree twenty yards or so away. Max circled the tree, barking wildly, as if trying to figure out how to climb it himself, but his prey had disappeared.

"They're gone, ya silly dog. Now come!" He let out a few more yaps before staring in my direction, his pink tongue lolling out of his mouth. "Come on! We gotta go!"

He darted toward me, tail wagging.

The noise of a fast-approaching engine flew to me on the wind. No one in their right mind would drive down this road at that speed. It was suicidal—the curves were too sharp, and a deer could jump in front of you at any time.

Or a dog, I thought as Max placed a paw on the road.

"Max, STAY," I screamed. "Go back!"

The driver didn't brake, hesitate, or otherwise acknowledge that he had noticed either Max or me. I leapt back in horror as a pickup truck sped between us creating a blast of wind so strong that, although it wouldn't have troubled a human, it nearly lifted me into it, causing me to flit away to some unknown destination. Even worse, the cloud of dust it kicked up blocked my view of Max.

My breath shook with fear, terrified of what I might see when the dust settled. I picked up a rock and flung it at the truck, but it missed, and the stone fell to the ground with a thud.

I glared at the pickup as it sped away, too scared of looking over and seeing Max splattered across the road, I watched as the truck's front tire hit a deep pothole as it rounded the next curve, tossing the loosely packed junk in the bed of the truck. A bag spilled off the top and rolled down the bank. The driver didn't seem to notice as he squealed out of sight.

A wet nose and a warm, wiggling body rubbed

against my legs. Relief burst through me. I took a few deep breaths to calm my pounding heart.

"Max, how many times do I have to tell you? The squirrels will be the death of you one of these days!" I scolded as I scooped up the cocker spaniel and held him close to my thumping heart.

My ire rose again as my eyes landed on the bag that had fallen from the truck. I put the dog down and stomped over to it, Max trotting beside me. *He nearly kills us, then just leaves his junk on the road. Some nerve!*

I lifted the black bag, surprised by its weight. It was an old scuffed up backpack with two main compartments and a couple of side pockets. A long zipper ran along the top of the bag and a second secured the compartment on the bottom. I partially unzipped the top and glanced inside to discover a jumble of strange bright orange envelopes. Curious, I lifted one out and opened it to find a bunch of printed photographs and strips of negatives inside. The photographs were old and worn, showing the effects of being handled, shuffled around and shown off.

Photographs never looked sharply focused to my Sidhe eyes, but it was easy to assess that the images were family photos focused mainly on a small boy of four or five.

A plastic label dangled from the lower zipper. A quick glance identified the bag's owner: Walter Strum. Good; I would go tell Mr. Strum exactly what I thought of his driving.

On closer inspection I noticed the address listed on the tag as well, a place in town not that far from the Apple Dumpling Café.

"Shit," I said under my breath as I remembered how late I was. I should have been at the café half an hour ago. I tossed the backpack over my shoulder and sprinted back to my car. Max, for once, followed obediently at my heels.

CHAPTER 2

I stood outside the back door of the café, FedEx box and toolbox in hand, using my heightened Sidhe senses to try to decipher what awaited me on the other side. I heard dishes clanging and voices humming as clearly as if I were in the room, but nothing that warned that a firestorm awaited me. Confidence bolstered, I eased the door open and snuck inside with the crazy idea that I might succeed in fixing the dishwasher before Mrs. Krauss discovered I was there.

I had barely closed the door behind me when Ida Krauss, the stocky, crotchety, gray-haired owner of the Apple Dumpling Café, blocked my path. A mere five foot two inches tall, she glared up at me with her tight-fisted hands on her hips.

"You promised you would be here an hour ago, young lady," she said, voice curt. "*Before* the morning rush."

"Seven o'clock is early! I mean, who gets up that early?" I asked, practically stuttering. Her eyebrows shot up as she glanced back toward the dining room. It was packed, bustling with people chatting on their phones or checking their email as they stood waiting in line for their morning coffee.

"I, er, had some trouble with Max," I said, trying a new tactic.

"You can't bring that dog in here. You'll get me a health code violation," she said, scanning the floor for him.

I sighed. "I know, Mrs. K. You've told me that a million times. He's not here, he's outside."

" I don't know how you can run your own business and be this irresponsible," she said, shaking her head. "I should have known better than to rely on a child."

I bit my lip to stop myself from reminding her for the thousandth time that I was a grown woman. The Sidhe live longer and age slower than humans, the result being that most people mistake me for a teenager. I'm 27 years old.

"That machine is too old to fix, anyway," she continued her rant. "Should've just bought a new one the day it broke down."

"Now that I have the part I need, I'll have it fixed in a minute," I said, lifting the box to illustrate my point. "I've kept your appliances running for the past six months, right? I won't let you down now."

"Sure hope not," she said, waving dismissively toward the broken appliance. "And stop with all that Mrs. K nonsense. Ida. Call me Ida, for heaven's sake!" she grumbled before stomping off to harass her staff members waiting on customers.

The rich, welcoming aroma of coffee permeated the

air, making my mouth water. As tempting as it was, I told myself I had I'd better do my job before grabbing a cup or I would risk reigniting Ida's wrath.

Emma Rodgers, a pretty, twenty-something strawberry-blond, stood at the basin next to the dishwasher, her long curls were stuffed into a hairnet. She was handwashing an overflowing pile of dishes with a bitter expression. She grumbled in my direction as I approached.

"Emma," I said.

"Sloan. I'm glad you're here. Finally." She shook her gloved hands, sending drops of water into the sink.

"Why is she making you wash the dishes?"

"She's been riled up all morning—because of you, I might add."

"Yeah, sorry about that." My face flushed with embarrassment, even though I knew she was just giving me a hard time. "Hey Em, don't worry about washing the rest. I'll have this thing up and running in a minute. I'll run the rest of those dishes through the machine when I'm done."

"You got a deal," she grinned, letting the water drain from the sink. She tugged off her rubber gloves and massaged her wrist. "My arm's killing me."

"I can't believe it still hurts. Hasn't it been months since your fall?"

"It only bothers me when I overuse it, it's fine," she said, brushing off my concern.

"If you're done socializing, there are pies that won't make themselves," Ida called from across the room, looking pointedly at Emma.

My friend looked at me and sighed. "You see, she's in a mood. I better get moving."

I glanced around at the other two women busy in the kitchen filling breakfast orders, no doubt they were unhappy with me as well. My only chance of redemption at this point was to fix the dishwasher as fast as possible. I opened my toolbox and got started.

"Get a new machine," I muttered, shaking my head as I unscrewed the side panel. It was an empty threat on Ida's part and I knew it, but it still annoyed me. The several thousand dollars it would cost to buy a new commercial dishwasher would stretch Ida's wallet to the breaking point

This appliance might be twenty years old, but it was in perfectly good condition. After I replaced the heating elements and performed some routine maintenance, it would be almost like new. People were so quick to get rid of perfectly good machinery!

Forty-five minutes later, I settled into my usual chair in the dining room and took a big gulp, then a second, of a deliciously perfect blend of cream and dark roast coffee. My table, strategically chosen, was in the far corner of the café where I could sit with my back to the wall and a good view of all the other customers in the place.

The crowd had thinned as the workday began, leaving behind a hodgepodge of locals and tourists visiting the Pocono Mountains. The line at the register had shrunk down to a quarter of what it had been when I arrived.

I let my gaze sweep over the dozen or so people who sat enjoying their breakfast. By now I recognized the regulars, residents of Findale who frequented the café early in the morning. They greeted each other warmly and shared conversations, hunching across tables, nursing hot coffee or tea and munching on the café's famous pastries.

The only form of acknowledgment I received from the regulars was a cautionary side look. Although my glamour camouflages my pearlized skin, the metallic sheen to my hair and my pointed ears, making me appear human, the flower tattoos around my neck and my short purple hair stand out, making me eccentric in their eyes. They had gotten used to my presence and seemed to accept that I wasn't a threat after I'd breakfasted here every day for the last six months, but that's as far as it had gone.

I doubted they would ever accept me as one of them. I snickered; if they only knew the truth in that sentiment. Then again, they don't even believe that the fae really exist.

Honestly, staying in my neutral corner suited me fine. I preferred to live anonymously.

My gaze roved around the room, landing for a moment on a stranger leaning against the wall close to the door. He neither joined the line nor took a seat. He was staring hard at me; a typical reaction. I stared back. Most people would avert their gaze, embarrassed by their own rude behavior, but not this guy. He continued pitting his stare with mine, causing me to squirm.

Something about his expression made me feel exposed, like he could see through my glamour to the real me. I reached up and fiddled with the amethyst earrings piercing the edge of my right ear, relieved to find them still there. My glamour, anchored by the natural energy from the stones, was still in place.

The café door swung open, distracting me from the stranger. Tommy Lynch strode in. His navy police uniform played up his sea blue eyes and his crop of thickly curled hair looked slightly tousled from the breeze.

Tommy had always been popular with the locals; they called out greetings to him as he passed. He smiled and waved in response. An older woman with salt and pepper hair stopped him as he was passing her table.

"Is it true about the Newburg sisters?" she asked.

"Yes, I'm sorry to say," Tommy responded, the lopsided smile melting from his face as he shook his head sadly.

"Gladys, didn't you believe me?" Ida asked, setting a plate of fruit and a toasted English muffin in front of her. "I told you—they say it was a suicide pact."

"What's this?" one of the regulars asked. "Something happened to Will and Susan's girls?"

"They both killed themselves last night. OD'd, it seems," chimed in Evelyn, another friend of Ida's who was sitting beside Gladys.

"That's just so tragic," said another local.

"That's exactly why I was hoping Tommy would tell me it wasn't true. Those poor parents lost both their girls in one awful night." Gladys blew her nose loudly.

"And nobody suspected a thing, from what I heard," Ida said with a frown. She set another plate in front of Evelyn and headed back to the kitchen.

Tommy inched away from the ladies while the conversation bounced around, seemingly eager to make his escape. I shook my head. Even with such a grim story, the women's love of gossip prevailed. To them, the only thing better then spreading stories around town was beating each other to the punch. He wandered my direction as he waited for his coffee.

"Hey kid, staying out of trouble?" he asked.

"I'm not a kid," I corrected, miffed. He chuckled.

"What about the staying out of trouble part?"

I chose to ignore his teasing and drained my coffee cup dry, eager to refill it and grab breakfast. Before I could stand, Ida appeared next to me. She slid a plate of bacon, eggs and toast onto the table.

"Now, I want to see you eat this up."

"Wow, this is way too much. I'll just grab my usual donuts," I said, eyeing the food dubiously.

"You're too skinny, even with all those sweets you gobble up. Probably because you're so tall," she said, crossing her arms; a sign she was putting her foot down. "You're obviously not eating enough. I only see you at breakfast, but at least I can make sure you have one good meal a day."

I looked up at her, ready to argue. Her pale blue eyes glared down at me, daring me to contradict her. I drew in a deep breath and sighed. Why bother? No one ever won an argument with Ida Krauss. I picked up a fork and took a bite of scrambled eggs.

"Mrs. K, I mean, Ida, do you know someone named Walter Strum? " I asked, changing the subject.

"Only for the last thirty plus years," she said. "Why do you ask?"

"I found a backpack earlier. Name tag says it belongs to him," I said, shrugging as if it were no big deal. "I want to return it."

She eyed me as she wiped down the counter. "He's the pharmacist at the drugstore on Church Street. He owns the place, too."

I leaned back in my chair, surprised. "You mean that guy who looks like Santa Claus?"

Ida nodded. "That's him alright. White beard, round belly." She grinned and her eyes became slits. "As a matter of fact, he dons the red suit every year for the church's Christmas party. The kids love him."

"So Church Street is his business address? I assumed it would be his home address," I said, revising my mental image.

"Well he practically lives there, what with the hours he puts in. Such a hard worker! His home is a couple of blocks away."

"I guess that's why he put the store address on the name tag. Does he drive a red pickup?"

"He doesn't drive at all since he had a stroke, maybe five years ago." She frowned, waving a cotton rag in my face. "What's this all about?"

I shrugged. I wondered what this was all about myself. What had his backpack been doing in the back of someone else's truck?

CHAPTER 3

I grabbed an extra-large cup of coffee to go and called out goodbyes to Ida, Emma, and the rest of the crew. Max yapped excitedly as I stepped out of the back door. He stood on the driver's seat of the Mustang, his front paws draped over the edge of the glass of the half-opened window. His entire head stuck out through the opening. I grinned at the comical picture his antics made.

"Told you I wouldn't be too long," I said, scratching him behind a floppy ear.

Expertly balancing the big paper cup, I opened the door to let Max escape and rolled up all four windows. The backpack had fallen over, dumping some of its contents across the Mustang's back seat. Not wanting to risk spilling even a drop of delicious nectar, I placed my coffee gingerly on the roof of the car, making sure it was balanced before stuffing the envelopes back into the bag and flinging it over my shoulder. I locked the doors, retrieved the coffee and headed down the alley with Max at my ankle.

The autumn air had a nip to it. I strode down Church Street past St. Francis Church, sipping coffee to keep warm while looking for the address on the backpack's label. Five blocks further on I spotted a worn canopy over the doorway of a storefront across the street. Its maroon fabric had faded so much that the words *'Strum's Pharmacy'* in white lettering were barely legible.

"There it is," I said, talking to myself as much as to the dog.

We made a beeline for the shop, jaywalking across the street in the process. I slowed as I stepped onto the sidewalk in front of the store. The pharmacy looked dark and closed. The neon open sign in the window was off, as were the interior lights. Convinced the place was closed, I was about to retrace my steps back to the car when I noticed that the door was ajar. I nudged it open a few more inches, blanching as a familiar metallic odor hit me from inside: blood.

Max charged inside before I could stop him. I hesitated on the threshold, cursing a blue streak. I had promised myself when I left The Otherworld that I would build a simple, uncomplicated life here and stay out of the spotlight. I took a deep breath and exhaled in a huff. Somebody could have fallen and hurt themselves... or something more sinister could have happened. Suddenly it seemed that I had little choice but to get caught up in someone else's drama.

I glanced down and knew without a doubt that something violent had happened. The long, narrow, deadly head of *Lugh's Spear* lay at my feet. One of the four ancient treasures of my people, the spear had chosen me as its bearer. I ignored it when it first turned up, unaware of its history or powers, until a friend and fellow Sidhe put the pieces together for me. The blade materialized whenever I was in danger, disappearing again once the threat had passed. Others had tried to claim it, but it always found its way back to me.

"Max, get out here," I hissed, bending to scoop up the blade by its four-inch handle. I had no connection with this pharmacist guy; never even met him, for that matter. I tried to tell myself that we could still just walk away, but I knew deep down that I couldn't leave when someone might need my help. Max had yet to reappear, so I pushed the door open and tiptoed inside.

The air in the tiny store was unusually still. Only the dim buzz of electricity radiating from a refrigerator on the far wall disturbed the silence. I slid the backpack off my shoulder and dropped it soundlessly onto the floor, dumping my coffee cup into a nearby trash bin to free up my fighting arm. I squared my stance, tightening my grip on my weapon as I assessed the situation.

No one cried out for help or moaned in pain. There was no movement, and there was no sign of Max. There was only the eerie glow of the light behind the pharmacy counter and the overpowering stench of blood.

Max's high-pitched bark broke the silence.

"Max?" I called, sprinting toward the back of the store. I skidded to a stop as he trotted out from behind the counter, leaving a track of dark footprints in his wake. Blood covered his paws and the fur along the bottom of his stomach, changing its golden color to a sickening crimson red. "Oh my god, are you hurt?"

I was reaching out to grab him when my foot hit the trail of blood, sending me flying. My butt slammed against the floor, sending a burst of pain up my back.

"Damn it!" I muttered under my breath.

I twisted into a kneeling position and grabbed for Max again, desperate to inspect him for wounds. He squirmed away from me, shaking himself as he trotted into the pharmacy area and back again as if coaxing me to follow.

I pushed myself up to a low crouch, spearhead in hand. I skimmed my fingertips along the wall to help me keep my balance on the blood-smeared floor as I crept around the pharmacy counter. I doubted anyone else was here, but I didn't want to take any chances. Someone could be unconscious back there—or lying in wait to claim another victim.

Max's panting disrupted the quiet as he danced beside me, trying to figure out what game we were play-ing. I took a deep breath to ground myself. Whatever—or whoever—I found on the other side... well, it wouldn't be good. I rounded the corner.

Walter Strum lay face up on the white tile floor in a pool of blood, eyes wide and mouth gaping open. Dark, reddish-brown stains covered the front of his pale blue smock. No need to rush over to help him or even feel for a pulse; he was clearly dead.

Chaos surrounded him. A shelving unit had been knocked over, littering the floor with pill bottles, broken glass, capsules and tablets. A wire basket that had held white bags of filled prescriptions been knocked down, its contents scattered.

I straightened up, keeping my guard up as I scanned the store again. Whoever had done this must have fled.

Water sprang to my eyes, but I forced my tears to stay put by shear willpower. I thought I had left scenes like this behind when the Unseelie war ended and I left The Otherworld. Memories flooded my brain, bloody battlefields, lost loved ones. Suddenly the need to get out of that place and away from the stench of the coppery smell of blood overwhelmed me. I grabbed Max's collar and dragged him outside.

The whole thing seemed surreal out in the bright morning sunlight, but a glance down at the mess Max had made of me made it all too real. Red stains covered my jeans and the bottom of my t-shirt. My hands were sticky with blood from my attempt to check Max for injuries. I wiped them on the sides of my ruined pants. Even the spearhead was splattered with blood.

I jumped as a car door slammed nearby, suddenly noticing the harsh red and blue lights flashing in the street.

"Sloan! Are you hurt?" called Tommy as he ran towards me, his pace slowing when he noticed the blood-splattered blade in my hand.

"No," I shook my head, resigning myself to what his arrival meant for me. There was no turning back; I was officially involved. "But the guy inside can't say the same. It's Walter Strum, and he's dead."

"Sloan, give me the knife," said Tommy, reaching out slowly as if not wanting to spook me. The blade of the spear was often mistaken for an odd shaped knife, since humans rarely saw spears. My brows knit as I considered his cautious attitude. I twisted my wrist and passed him the spear, handle first.

"You think *I* did this?"

CHAPTER 4

"What happened? Did he come after you? Try to hurt you?" Tommy asked as multiple police cruisers came screeching in on the street in front of us. Max was leaning against my leg, yapping at the commotion while his little body trembled. I scooped him up into my arms.

"What are you accusing me of? I just came here to return a backpack I found with his name on it."

"What backpack?"

I shook my head; this guy was unbelievable. At least he had assumed it had been self-defense.

"It's inside. Tommy, he was dead when I got here."

He stared at me for several seconds. "It's better to tell the truth now than to change your story later."

I gritted my teeth and stared back. I refused to repeat that I was innocent.

A graying African American police officer took Lugh's Spear from him with gloved hands. He placed it into a clear plastic bag which he then sealed and took away.

"What's he going to do with it?" I asked.

"Forensics will need to test the knife to see if it matches the murder weapon. You'll get it back when they're done," Tommy said.

"Hmm," I raised an eyebrow. The spear came and went as it pleased. Inevitably, at some point they would go looking for it and find it gone. Imagining their reaction would be funny, if the consequence of potentially damning evidence disappearing wasn't sure to throw more suspicion onto me. I bit my lip to hold back a groan.

The bustle of police activity had attracted people from the surrounding homes and businesses. For every person who ventured outside for a closer look, at least one more was gawking through the windows. Just the kind of attention I came to this town to avoid.

A chubby, balding man in a suit pushed through the onlookers, making his way to the closest police officer. He conferred with her for a few moments and then beckoned to Tommy.

He looked at me, his expression grave. "Stay here. Don't try to leave; you'll just get yourself into more trouble," he said before walking over to the man. The two of them turned their backs to me as they huddled for a private conversation. Despite their caution, I easily eavesdropped on their conversation.

"I understand you were first on the scene," Baldy stated.

"Yes, sir."

"What are we looking at?"

"The victim was stabbed multiple times. The place was ransacked, so possible robbery. The state forensics team is in there now collecting—"

"Ms. Murray." I jumped again and huffed in disgust that I had been caught off-guard. It was the graying policeman again; I should have heard him coming. "I'm Officer Clark. You and the dog need to come with me."

He took me by the elbow and escorted me to the back seat of his patrol car, Max still in my arms. "Wait here," he said, not unkindly. He closed the car door and hurried to stop a young man from entering the store—*the crime scene*, I corrected myself.

"Whoa, you can't go in there!" Clark called out.

"You don't understand, I work here," said the young man.

"What I don't understand is how you got past the perimeter." He glared at the officer who should have stopped the guy, but her back was to him and she didn't notice.

"Listen, my boss has insane rules about being late. I'll lose my job—"

"You don't need to worry about that right now."

I hugged Max tight, my stomach aching from the stress of the last hour. His presence was comforting, despite his sticky matted fur. He had worn himself out and had finally stopped barking.

More police arrived, raising their number to six or seven. Who knew this tiny town even had so many police officers? Tommy was still speaking to the chubby man who appeared to be in charge. I could have listened in if

I had concentrated, but I lacked the energy to make the effort. Besides, Tommy's body language told me everything I needed to know.

I sighed and looked away, surveying the surrounding crowd instead. Many of the people stared back at me, the girl with the purple hair and tattoos sitting in the back seat of the police car. Presumably they were all under the impression that I was the murderer. *How did I get myself into this stupid situation?* I clamped down the urge to jump out of the vehicle and flit away as the desire to flee swept over me. I put a hand on Max, reminding myself that I couldn't leave him behind. I sank lower in the seat, hoping in vain that dropping out of their eyesight would make me feel better. It didn't.

I switched tactics, turning my attention to the only people who weren't staring at me. Two men stood off to the side, ignoring the bustle around them. Facing me was the same guy Clark had stopped from running into the pharmacy. He was dark-haired and clean-cut in a button-down dress shirt, and he appeared to be in his mid to late twenties. He leaned against the building, arms folded over his chest.

The other man faced away from me. His stiff back and jerky movements were telltale signs that he was angry. Judging by his white lab coat, he was probably a doctor or another pharmacist. I stretched my senses to listen to their argument. Between the noisy street and the closed car, it was hard to make out much more than the hiss of anger in Lab Coat's voice. Concentrating hard, I managed to pick up a few words.

"If they figure out—"

Officer Clark opened the door and slid into the

driver's seat, making just enough noise to drown out the remainder of the sentence.

"We need to take your statement, but the crowd here's getting too large. I'm going to drive you down to the station."

"Whether or not I want to go?"

"Ah, come on now. You want to cooperate, don't you?" he asked, glancing over his shoulder at me before turning the key and inching out onto Church Street.

We traveled in silence while I stewed over how much I did *not* want to cooperate. We reached police headquarters' parking lot ten minutes later.

*M*ax's paws hit the macadam seconds after Clark opened the back door. Growling, he charged at an approaching man wearing scrubs. The guy flinched and took a quick step backward.

"That dog should be on a leash," he grumbled. Max stopped a few feet away from him, barking furiously.

I shrugged as I scooped him up again and shushed him. "He's not gonna hurt anyone. He just likes to act tough."

"Well, we need some way to control him so I can take him to the lab to collect samples."

"What? No. You're not taking my dog."

"They'll need to test the blood on him, along with his hair and anything else forensics might need," Clark said. He cut me off as I started to protest. "They won't hurt him. Cooperation, remember? As a matter of fact, we'll need to take the clothes you're wearing too."

· · ·

*T*hey rummaged around and found some things for me to change into, taking away the clothes I'd had on and sitting me in a tiny room with no windows. At 5'9 I tended to be taller than most women, but the clothes' previous owner must have been not only shorter but curvier than me. Somehow, the t-shirt and sweats managed to feel too small and too large at the same time. The room I was in was barely larger than a closet, the cool institutional green of the walls making it feel cold, stark, and unfriendly.

So this is an interrogation room, I thought. There was no two-way mirror along the wall like on TV, but a camera hung in the corner, no doubt recording my every move.

I wrapped myself up tight, folding my arms across my chest and crossing one knee over the other to contain the anger that threatened to explode from within me. I shook my head, disgusted with myself for allowing them to take Max away.

I unfolded myself as the door creaked open. Baldy, the man who had been speaking with Tommy outside the pharmacy, strode in and slammed the door behind him.

"I'm Detective Moody," he said. I smirked. Moody was a perfect name for this dumpy looking, sallow complexion guy who I suspected never smiled. His tie was askew and fell two inches short of the bottom of his pudgy stomach and his skin had an odd lumpiness to it.

Moody sneered, recognizing the disrespect in my expression and repaying it in kind.

"Where's Max?" I asked.

"Who's Max, a co-conspirator?" We stared at each

other in a standoff. I refused to respond to his baiting question; he had to know Max was a dog.

"Why'd you do it?" he asked, changing tactics.

"I didn't *do* anything. I just found the guy."

"You're covered in his blood, you had a weapon in your hand also covered in blood and Officer Lynch practically caught you in the act. If he had arrived a few seconds earlier, that's exactly what would have happened."

I shook my head. Suddenly I couldn't stand the sight of him. I fixed my gaze on the ugly green wall instead.

"Listen, I already told Tommy and two other cops: I just wanted to drop off a backpack I'd found. I saw all the blood, so I took out my knife for protection and went inside to see if anybody needed help. Max splattered the blood all over everything. Find the guy driving the red pickup; chances are, he's the killer."

He chuckled and shook his head, his disbelief obvious.

"Why would I kill him? I didn't even know the guy!"

Moody's face twisted into a smug grin. He threw the backpack on the table, unzipping the lower compartment. The top tumbled over, exposing the bundles of hundred-dollar bills stashed inside.

"Money. The oldest motive in the book."

"I must be some kind of weird thief to be taking the loot back," I said, laughing off my shock at how easily he was building a case against me.

Moody's face flushed red with anger, but I refused to let him see a crack in my devil-may-care facade.

"There was a streak of shoplifting a few years ago. Unsolved, but you were the top suspect. This time you were out for bigger stakes. You tried to rob the pharmacy, but Walter caught you in the act and you panicked."

"That's a nice theory, Detective, but I had nothing to do with either incident." We glared at each other; teeth clenched. Ida's furious voice drifted down the hallway outside the door a moment later.

"How dare you interrogate that girl? She's just a child!"

"Come on, Ida, you know we have to follow procedure," Tommy said. "We'll need to speak to all the involved parties before we're done."

"Thomas Lynch, don't you try to tell me that's a friendly little chat going on in there. Even if it is, that baby shouldn't be in there alone!" Ida threw open the door and stomped in like an avenging angel.

"Well now, Joseph. I can't imagine what your wife will think about your behavior here, once I tell her all about it. How dare you interrogate this child without an adult present?"

The detective drew in a deep breath and sighed, turning towards Ida. "I'm just doing my job. She's not a child; her driver's license says she's twenty-seven."

"Oh please, look at that face. I'd be surprised if she's a day over sixteen!" She thrust her hand out toward me. "Come on, honey. Let's get out of here."

I took her hand and smiled sweetly at Moody. Would he actually try to fight the indomitable Ida Krauss?

"I don't have enough to hold you now, but don't leave town," he told me, his fury evident in his voice. "We're not done with you."

CHAPTER 5

*I*da pulled her car into the gravel driveway in front of my home and slid the gear into park. Her gaze swept the rusty exterior of my battered trailer, still a work in progress. My refurbishing thus far was only visible on the inside.

"I hate leaving you here on your own. You should come back to the café with me," she repeated for the hundredth time.

I pressed my lips together to stifle an angry outburst. She had refused to take me to the café earlier, when I'd wanted to get my car and drive myself home. We ended up arguing for the entire ride out of Findale after she decided she wanted to take me back to the café after all, by which point I'd had enough. I exhaled slowly, reminding myself that she was just trying to be nice.

"Don't worry about me, I'll be fine. Besides, Max desperately needs a bath, and he can't be in the café even on his best day. I'll be over in the morning as usual." Ida glanced at the dog and wrinkled her nose.

"Okay, but if I don't see you at your regular time, I will send out a search party," she threatened. I nodded and jumped out of the car before she could start another round. Then, hesitating, I turned around to ask the question that had been bothering me since we'd left the station.

"Ida, you know I'm not underage, don't you?"

She tilted her head and thought for a minute before she spoke. "To my heart you're a poor motherless child, all alone in the world. But that's just my maternal instincts kicking into overdrive. My head knows you're an adult, but why not milk that baby face for as long as you can? Before you know it, you'll be old like me."

She gave me a wink and a conspiratorial smile before shifting into reverse and backing out of the driveway. I waved as her car sped down the road towards town. As much as I liked to complain about her, I still blessed the day my friend and mentor, Tressa, had asked her to look after me.

As she disappeared around the bend, I sank onto the stairs in front of the trailer door and dropped my head into my hands. I rubbed my fingers over my forehead, trying to relieve a developing headache. *What a day.*

Max poked his snout up between my knees and licked my chin, forcing me to smile even as I reeled away from the offensive odor radiating from him. I didn't want to take him inside like this and have my home reeking as well, so I retrieved a big plastic tub and a huge bottle of pet shampoo from inside the trailer that I had bought to deal with the smelly messes he seemed to find everywhere. Suffice it to say, this wasn't the first time Max had gotten himself into a dirty mess.

I lifted him into the tub and struggled to hold him there while soaking him with the hose. The water pooling in the tub was a nasty rust color. The dollop of shampoo I squirted into my palm would never be enough for this mess. On second thought, I squeezed a long line of shampoo down the length of his back, letting the soap cascade down his blood-soaked fur. I set the bottle on the ground and began lathering him up, starting with his stump of a tail.

As I worked, I thought back over the conversation at the police station. Moody had made a convincing case against me. Truth be told, I *was* the one behind the shoplifting spree, although whether I had stolen anything or not was debatable.

What I hadn't known back then was that the Sidhe have an innate ability to hold *Dominion* over anyone they can true name, forcing them to do whatever you tell them to do. Unlike the Sidhe, humans give up their true name easily. I noticed a pattern as I was growing up, if I said someone's name before asking for something, they always gave it to me. All I had to do was get the store owner's name, look them in the eye and ask them to give me whatever item I was after, which they inevitably did. Unfortunately, not only did they not have a choice, but they didn't remember doing it.

I'd had no idea that I could control other people's wills; I had been raised as a human. Of course, I knew I was different from everyone around me—I mean, no one else had pointy ears, and no one else noticed mine. I didn't find out I was a Sidhe until I met Tressa just a few years earlier. She was the one who explained to me that I was holding *Dominion* over people and taking away their free will, which is a terrible thing to do and illegal by fae law. Once I understood, I did my best to make amends.

I worked my hands down the length of Max's body, rubbing the shampoo into his fur until I reached his long floppy ears. Only his little face was free of soap. He chose that moment to shake out his coat, covering me with filthy suds.

"Hey! I'll take my shower inside, thank you," I teased.

I wiped the soap from my face with a towel as my mind returned to the its unpleasant contemplation of my current situation. I weighed my options. I could run, either back to Faery or somewhere else in the Human World.

Although there were a handful of people I could count on in The Otherworld, I was an even bigger outcast in Faery than I was in Findale. People there see me either as the Bearer of Lugh's Spear—too far out of their reach to befriend—or the Unseelie with the awful tattoos—too far beneath them to bother with and unworthy of this odd accolade. I had no control over these things and they hardly defined me as a person, but there wasn't a lot I could do about it.

Lugh's Spear, the *Gae Assail,* had chosen me to be its bearer. I had no idea what it was the first time I tripped over it. The Seelie and Unseelie factions of the Sidhe people had waged war against each other for centuries, fighting over control of The Otherworld and the four treasures of their people. I didn't choose to be born Unseelie, but for many of the Sidhe, it didn't seem to matter that I had converted and fought for the good guys. As for the tattoos—well, that was their problem, not mine.

I felt much more comfortable here in Findale, living off the beaten path and getting close to only a small number of people who were willing to learn who I am as a person—well, except the part about being a Sidhe.

Starting over in a new location in the human world was just as unappealing, especially if the police were after me. Besides, I'd promised Tressa that I would look after Pine Ridge, the estate where I parked my trailer. Pine Ridge belonged to her, and I didn't want to lose ties with her and my other friends in Faery.

I made my decision as I took up the hose for Max's final rinse: I would not run, but I couldn't rely on the police to find the guilty party. I had done nothing wrong, but Moody had already decided that I was guilty. I would have to figure out who had killed the pharmacist and clear my name myself. Despite Ida's good intentions running interference for me, there was no one else I could trust to get out me of this mess. No one else would have my back.

I toweled Max dry and tried to work the brush through his tangled fur, but he refused to cooperate. *Everything about this day has been harder than it should have been*, I moaned silently.

"Come on, Maxie, we're almost done," I pleaded, gripping him firmly to try to keep him still. Suddenly, his tail began to wag furiously. I stopped brushing mid-stroke as a familiar phrase floated to me on the wind: '*Bláth Dorcha.*' I hadn't heard that name in months.

The voices were coming from the forest behind the trailer. I was able to hear them directly as the newcomers came closer, no longer needing the wind to carry their words to me. The heaviness that lay over me lifted when I recognized the voice of one of my good friends from The Otherworld. I hurried over to the edge of the yard to welcome the new arrivals.

Free of restraint, Max bolted past me and into the trees. A second later he reemerged, dancing around two Leprechauns. The first was a fully grown man, four feet tall with a dark beard, a balding head and a mandolin hanging across his back. He was holding the hand of a fair-haired, freckle-faced boy half his height.

The boy broke free and ran to me, his eyes wide with excitement. "You're her! The great *Bláth Dorcha*." He bowed at the waist, sweeping his hands out dramatically.

"None of that now," I admonished, touching his shoulder to encourage him to straighten. *Bláth Dorcha*—which translates to Dark Flower—was a name I had acquired in The Otherworld, where my tattoos were even more unusual than they were in Findale. My stint of notoriety as the Dark Flower is what convinced me that a quiet, inconspicuous life suited me best.

"Is this Max?" the boy asked, his voice lifting a few notes higher. He forgot me in an instant, dropping to one knee to pet the dog.

"Cormac, what on earth are you doing here?" I asked, my heart swelling with happiness as I leaned over to hug him. His timing couldn't have been better. "And who is this you've brought with you?"

"We Leprechauns didn't like you being here on your own. We swore an oath to protect you, but prudence dictated that we should not all come into the Human World together." I nodded in agreement. Cormac was part of a group of warrior Leprechauns who had fought with me in The Otherworld during the final Unseelie war. Leprechaun glamour made humans see them as Little People. A sudden influx of a dozen of them to our small community would be sure to draw unwanted attention, something the fae tried to avoid whenever possible.

"The war is over; there's no need to protect me now," I said, which was true… but if it motivated him to come visit me here, I wasn't going to complain.

"You saved our lives. There isn't an expiration on that debt."

I shook my head. Experience had taught me that arguing a debt of honor with a Leprechaun was useless. I gestured towards my yard, inviting them in. "So everyone is okay then?" I asked as we strolled towards the camper.

"Aye, we've all returned to our trades. We've set up shop at the village around Castle Conall; we're rebuilding our lives, as it were. Some more so than others," he said, his voice wistful. I glanced at him; his tone suggested he hadn't done as well in his effort to rebuild. "It made the most sense for me to be the one to move here. Aside from wanting to check on you myself, I've spent more time among humans than the others."

"And this little guy?" I asked, nodding towards the boy. He and Max had run on ahead of us, absorbed in their games.

"My nephew, Padraig. We lost both his parents in the war, so he is my ward now. He has never been here before, of course, but he was most excited to meet the legendary Bl—"

"Don't. Not here. As long as we're in the Human

World, please just call me Sloan. We don't need anyone asking questions we can't answer."

He nodded. "Fair enough."

Padraig ran back to us, Max following at his heels. "What's that big metal box?" Padraig asked, pointing to the trailer.

"That would be my home," I said with a sigh. This was the second reminder in one day that to a stranger's eye, the trailer looked more like an oversized trash bin than a proper place to live.

*M*ost of the Sidhe start flitting as children, carefully supervised by their parents. I was a teenager the first time I rode the wind, and I did it completely by accident. It can be dangerous if you don't know what you're doing; you could just miss the edge of a cliff or careen into a tree if you don't know exactly where you want to land.

Flitting is even riskier in the Human World; you must be careful not to let anyone see you appearing or disappearing. I rarely flitted into town, especially in daylight; the risk of being caught was too great. With my Mustang still at the Café, I had little choice when it was time to make my way into Findale the next morning.

I flitted to a secluded section of woods in a park near the town center, a location I had scouted out long ago for just such situations. I ran a few steps to keep my balance as I came in; I hadn't yet mastered smooth landings. From there it was only a short two-block walk to the Café.

I stopped across the street from the building and watched the activity inside through the large plate-glass window in the front. The dining room was packed. Ida, coffee pot in hand, strolled among the tables refilling cups, commanding attention as she bantered back and forth with her patrons. It didn't take much to guess the topic of this morning's gossip.

After a moment's consideration, I walked one block further and turned into the alley behind the store. I'd become accustomed to entering through the back door from my many trips to fix appliances, and today didn't seem like the day to make a grand entrance through the front.

I jingled my car keys in my jeans pocket, thinking. I was tempted to hop in and drive away from the curiosity seekers inside, but I knew Ida would be true to her word. If I didn't show up, she would come looking for me.

I squared my shoulders and reached for the doorknob. These people wouldn't stop me from following my daily routine; I hadn't done anything wrong.

Emma was mixing a batter, somber faced when I came in. She turned off the machine when she saw me, wiping her hands on her apron as she hurried over to give me a quick hug.

"Are you okay? It must've been horrible, finding a dead body like that." I gave her a grim smile, grateful to her for assuming my innocence.

"Yeah, it wasn't pretty."

"I'm not sure you want to go out there," she said, nodding her head towards the dining room. "We made pumpkin muffins today, first of the season. Have one—

they're delicious, if I do say so myself. Eat it here in the kitchen, though."

"Thanks, maybe I will," I said, forcing a smile.

I grabbed an extra-large paper cup instead of my usual ceramic mug so I could take my coffee with me if at any point I decided to make a quick exit. Voices from the front of the café drifted into the kitchen as I opened the refrigerator and poured an inch and a half of heavy cream into the bottom of the cup.

"He wasn't that old, you know. Only seventy-two. The stroke aged him beyond his years, and he didn't have any family around to help him. I know he struggled to take care of himself," said Ida. Though I couldn't see her, I could easily imagine the look on her face: sadness mixed with a tinge of pride at being in the know.

"He had a daughter," Evelyn piped in. "She never came to visit though, even when he had a stroke and needed all the help he could get. I don't know how she lives with herself after treating her father that way. He always doted on her when she was a child."

"I mean seriously, who could have had anything against him? He was always smiling," said a voice I didn't recognize.

I filled the rest of my cup with coffee and sliced one of the pumpkin muffins in half, placing it in the toaster. I continued to eavesdrop while I waited, debating whether I should go to my regular table to eat my breakfast or take Emma's suggestion and stay back in the kitchen for a change.

"Was it a robbery? Or maybe his daughter is so messed up that *she* did it," Gladys speculated.

"He had multiple stab wounds—definitely a crime of passion."

"I heard it was that weird looking girl living out at Tressa's estate. They say he hurt her dog and she went nuts." *Here we go*, I thought with a frown.

The comforting aroma of pumpkin, cinnamon and walnuts filled the air as my muffin heated up. I spread a thick coat of butter over both sides when it was toasted, licking the runoff from my fingers. All the while, the conversation in the dining room continued.

"The police seem to think she did it, but not because of the dog. I heard she was looking for drugs and Walter surprised her."

"She's in here every day. Should we be worried?"

"She doesn't look like a killer. She would be so pretty if she did something with that purple hair and covered those tattoos."

I heard a loud clunk and a startled yelp as Ida slammed her coffee pot down. "What are you people thinking?" she scolded. "Sloan was here having breakfast right before she walked over to the pharmacy yesterday. Half of you saw her here. She found a bag with Walter's name on it and went over there to return it; she told me so before she left. She had nothing to do with this."

I smiled and gave her statement a jerky nod of approval. There was every possibility that Ida was milking her knowledge of the current hot gossip, but she did sound genuinely outraged. Her confidence in my innocence emboldened me. I shook my head to dishevel my hair—if they wanted wild, let's give them wild—picked up my muffin and strode into the dining room.

A hush fell over the crowd as I settled into my

regular table. The horde of gossips broke apart, trying to hide the fact that they had been talking about me by quickly starting innocuous conversations with the people around them. A few people stood and left.

"How are you doing this morning?" Ida asked as she rushed over. "Did you get any sleep?" She started to tip the coffee pot to refill my cup, righting it again when she realized it was still full.

"I'm fine. Please don't fuss," I said in a low voice. The last thing I wanted was for her to make a big to-do over me; I preferred to pretend everything was normal.

The café door opened and an unfamiliar woman entered. She wore a suit and carried a leather bag big enough to hold a laptop. She surveyed the interior of the café, taking in the botanical prints on the walls and scanning the tables before making her way to the counter.

"Well, as I live and breathe," Ida said under her breath before scurrying over to wait on the woman. "Tasha Strum, isn't it?"

"Lewis now. Haven't been a Strum for years. Hello, Mrs. Krauss. Looks like you've made some changes since I was a kid."

"Well! We haven't seen you around these parts for a long time. Where have you been hiding?"

"I haven't been hiding, I've been having a life. I live in Montclair now. New Jersey."

"Oh! Well, that's not *that* far away." I lifted my cup to my mouth to hide a grin. Ida had gotten a good dig in, but the woman either hadn't noticed or didn't care.

Ida took Tasha's order, placing a donut in a bag for her and pouring her tea.

"I'm so sorry about your father, dear," she said as she

passed the items over. "I'm assuming you're here to make arrangements?"

"Somebody has to do it," Tasha shrugged, pressing her lips into a thin straight line.

"I was wondering, what are you planning to do for food after the funeral?"

"I wasn't planning on anything. I just want to get the job done and go home."

The café had grown quiet as the other patrons strained to listen in, but a flurry of whispers burst out at this last comment.

"I see. I was going to offer the café, if you'd like; everyone can come here after the funeral and I'll pick up the tab. If you don't mind, that is."

"That would be fine, thank you," she said after a long hesitation, her expression slightly pained.

"Let me know the details once the funeral is arranged," said Ida. "Is there some way I can get in touch with you?"

"I'll be up at the pharmacy until I can figure out what to do with it," Tasha huffed, clearly annoyed to have to deal with this additional aspect of her father's death. She turned to leave, Ida watching her go with a furrowed brow.

"She used to be such a sweet girl..."

CHAPTER 7

I escaped from the café as soon as I finished my breakfast. The Mustang's engine roared for a moment before settling into a gentle purr. I put it in gear and eased down the alley onto Main Street.

I had promised to meet Cormac at my shop after breakfast. As I approached the old brick building, I saw a child standing on the hood of a parked car, hands on the windshield and butt in the air. I pulled up beside the car and a freckled face turned to smile at me.

"Padraig! What are you doing?"

"I wanted to see inside this thing."

"You can't stand on top of other people's cars. Get down from there!" He scooted across the hood toward me. "Not on this side, you could get hurt! Over there, on the sidewalk."

I closed my eyes and sighed as he ran across the hood of the car and jumped off. At least he was too small to have done any damage. He walked along the sidewalk, keeping pace with me as I looked for a parking spot scrutinizing the car's every movement. The moment I parked, he climbed the front bumper of the Mustang. I was out of the car in an instant, grabbing him around his waist before he could climb onto the hood and lowering his feet back down to the ground.

"You especially DO NOT climb on *my* car. Got it?" He nodded, pouting. A moment later he stood on his toes, cupping his hands around his eyes and pressing them to the passenger side window.

"There's a better way to see inside," I teased, opening the door for him. He hopped onto the black leather seat with his dirty shoes, fiddling with the knobs on the radio. I cringed but allowed him to explore. I sat down next to him as he scrambled over to the driver's seat, leaving the door hanging open.

"What *is* this thing?" he asked, gripping the stirring wheel and jerking it back and forth.

"Be careful! Treat her with respect."

Padraig dropped his hands, his eyebrows flying up. "This is an animal?"

"What? No." Then it hit me: he had never been in the Human World before. This was his first experience with a car. "It's a machine that gets you from one place to another. I'll take you for a ride later."

"You use machines to travel instead of dragons?"

"Shh," I said, glancing around to be sure no one was close enough to hear us. I pulled the door closed just in case. "Don't talk about things from The Otherworld out in the open. Didn't your uncle tell you that? You must never say or do anything to make the people here suspicious."

"Yes," he mumbled, hanging his head. "Sorry."

"Speaking of your uncle, where is he?"

He put his elbow on my shoulder and rested his chin in the palm of his hand. "He said the shop is a disgrace and he could never work in those conditions."

"He's in the store already?" I glanced over at the shop door. "How did he get in? I didn't give him a key."

"A key!" the little Leprechaun guffawed. "As if a plain old lock could stop Uncle Cormac."

I pulled the boy out of my car and stomped up to my shop. I had inherited the building from another Leprechaun who had used it to sell secondhand furniture. He had a unique gift for illusions, so he'd never bothered to fix up the dilapidated space. Instead, he simply masked its flaws with an illusion so effective that no one could see them. When he died, however, the illusion died with him. I didn't have that same talent; the building's faults and failings were clearly visible.

Thus far I had removed most of the old furniture and updated the electrical system and plumbing, but I hadn't painted the walls or done anything else cosmetic. The only other improvement I had made was to put a sign in the window that read "Murray's Appliance Repair: no machine too small or too big."

The front door opened into an airy, spacious showroom. My fix-it business only took up a corner of the store; it was a shop within a shop. Old sewing machines, mixers, vacuums, and televisions lined the shelving units I had installed along with a worktable, desk and checkout counter. More often than not, I made house calls to fix whatever appliance or gadget needed repairs. I'd never gotten any complaints from the people who came into the shop, so I hadn't made renovating a priority. Still, the insult from Cormac had stung.

A wooden plank cart sat in the middle of the room, loaded with musical instruments. Cormac stood beside it, hands on his hips as he examined the space. His Otherworld tunic, cinched at the waist with a leather belt and paired with matching pants, passed as bohemian on the musician, rather than fae.

"I can't display my instruments here. This place is a dump! It will detract from their beauty and drive customers away."

"Listen, Cormac," I snapped. "Humans have a saying: 'beggars can't be choosers.' If you plan to stay with me in Findale, this is your best option. You can fix it up any way you choose." I regretted the words as soon as they left my lips. I had let my hurt feelings get the best of me.

Cormac glared at me with fiery eyes; Leprechauns pride themselves on never taking charity. I held up my hands to stop him from exploding with anger.

"All I'm saying is that I'm willing to barter with you: your sweat equity in lieu of rent."

"I fix it up and get partial ownership," he countered.

I scrunched my face and shook my head, wanting to appear as though I was giving it serious consideration. Leprechauns love a tough negotiation; it would be the perfect way to soothe his ego.

"Twenty percent ownership. There's an apartment on the second floor; I'll make that part of the bargain. You and Padraig can live there rent free."

"Live in a building instead of a tree?" Padraig asked, incredulous.

"Fifty-fifty ownership. Even split, including the apartment."

"That's too much," I answered, walking around the cart of instruments as I looked at the paint peeling from the walls and the scruffy floors. "It just needs cosmetic work; the building is sound. Plus, there's a workroom in the back that still has all Gobban's woodworking tools. I'll throw them into the deal; they should be useful for making wooden instruments. I'll give you sixty-forty."

"Fifty-fifty."

I sighed, picking a flute out of the cart. The wood was smooth as silk, and he had carved an intricate Celtic knot along the sides. I played a quick scale on it; the sound was as smooth as the wood.

"I'll go fifty-fifty if you throw in this flute," I said, holding out a hand to shake on it. Cormac accepted and shook with me, looking quite satisfied with himself.

Negotiations over, the two of us relaxed onto a sofa that was pushed up against the far wall. Padraig left us alone and went off to explore the building.

"Have you been practicing?" Cormac asked, jutting his chin toward the instrument in my hands.

"No, I didn't bring my flute with me. I've missed it, though. We'll have to start up my lessons again."

"Aye, as soon as I get this place up to my standards. We should buy paint and get started right away," he said, beginning to stand. I put a hand on his arm to stop him.

"There's something I need to talk to you about first. I seem to be in a bit of trouble."

"What kind of trouble?" he asked, scowling.

"Yesterday I found the body of the local pharmacist;

47

he'd been stabbed to death. The police think I did it." No sense mincing words.

"Why? What reason would you have to kill this person?" He wrinkled his brow.

"There was a bag of money; they think I wanted to steal it. It didn't help that I was covered in blood, thanks to Max. So was my spearhead. They took me down to the police station for questioning and made it pretty clear that I was lucky to get out of there."

Cormac jumped to his feet. "They held you captive? Don't they know who you are?"

"No, Cormac, of course they don't know. They can't know."

"And the *Gae Assail*?"

"They took it for testing."

"*They took it*!" His face flushed bright red.

"Calm down, Cormac. Please. Once they test the blade, they'll see that it wasn't the murder weapon. That's my best shot for staying out of jail. That, or to figure out who really killed him."

"I will do everything I can to help you find this person. If they put you in jail I will break you out, just as you saved me and my brethren from the Unseelie prince. What can I do?"

"I don't have any real suspects yet, but he has a daughter. Her name is Tasha Lewis, from Montclair, New Jersey, and she doesn't seem at all sad that he's dead. She's as good a starting place as any. Would you mind taking a quick trip over to Montclair to see what you can learn about her?"

"I will go immediately. Padraig," he called. "Come; we have a mission."

CHAPTER 8

I leaned against the thick trunk of an old maple tree in St. Francis Cemetery, waiting for Walter Strum's funeral procession to arrive. It was a perfect autumn day: cool without being cold, the air crisp with the scent of newly fallen leaves. Colorful birds serenaded each other from the branches far above my head; soon they would fly south for the winter.

The peaceful serenity of my surroundings did wonders to soothe my jagged nerves. My mind felt freed from the endless whirl of worry that had been plaguing me for the last few days as I constantly wondered when the police would make their next move. Detective Moody hadn't come for me yet, but I often caught sight of one cruiser or another driving past my home and shop.

I'd been keeping an ear to the wind, but so far I hadn't heard anything floating around that pointed to the real killer. I had come to the interment to scout out the attendees, hoping to pick up some clues. Gladys had hinted at the daughter as a possible suspect; maybe her behavior would tell me something.

There were three fresh graves in the cemetery that day. Two of them were located side by side, each heaped high with recently turned mounds of dirt and with fading flower arrangements piled on top. This was the resting place of the Newburg sisters, whose sad end the gossips had chattered about at breakfast the other day. Those graves weren't my present concern.

I stood about fifteen yards away from the one grave that remained open, assuming it must have been prepared for Walter. I was close enough to get a good look at the mourners' faces, yet at a safe enough distance to keep from intruding on their grief.

The light sound of footsteps on the soft ground disrupted the surrounding peacefulness. I recognized the young man who came up behind me. I had seen him outside the pharmacy on the day of Walter's death, speaking with the doctor in the lab coat. He stood an inch or two taller than me; he wore his short brown hair slicked back from his handsome face and his clean-shaven chin sported an irresistible dimple. His suit fit smoothly across his broad shoulders. He stopped beside me, giving me an appreciative once over before settling his gaze on my eyes.

"Cool tats," he said.

"Thanks."

"Do you plan to move any closer?" he asked, nodding towards the open grave.

"No."

"Are you always this talkative?" he asked, grinning.

I made no response, watching as the hearse pulled

into the cemetery followed by a line of cars. The funeral director supervised two men as they unloaded the coffin, placing it on a metal frame with wheels. They rolled the coffin over to a spot prepared beside the open grave.

"You'd better get going. Looks like they're about to start," I said.

"Maybe I'll stay here with you."

I cocked my head, trying to guess his motives. "Someone over there must expect you. Were you family?"

"He was no family of mine," he said, glaring into the distance. "I worked for him at the pharmacy, that's all. I felt obligated to pay my respects, but... maybe the funeral service was enough." He shook his head as if trying to break free of his thoughts. He turned to meet my eyes. "My mother passed away several months ago. This is all too close, too familiar. It's taking me to a place I don't want to be."

I nodded; experience had taught me that the grief of losing a loved one can hit you when you least expected.

"Feel free to stay right here."

We waited together in silence, watching a man in a dark suit arranging flowers over the coffin. Mourners began to pour out of their cars, the men in dark suits and ties and the women all in black, gathering under the canopy beside the grave.

An impressive number of people had come to lay this man to rest. Ida sat in the middle row of the arranged chairs, her friends Evelyn and Gladys on either side. All three elderly ladies held hankies to mop their tears. I spotted several other café regulars sprinkled throughout the mourners. I almost missed Tommy where he stood in the back; he was wearing a suit instead of his uniform.

"I'm Jason, by the way," said the young man next to me.

"Sloan. Nice to meet you," I answered, ignoring the heat of his eyes on me. I kept my focus on the crowd around the gravesite instead. A group of three men stood off to the side, talking amongst themselves.

"Who are those men over there, do you know?" I asked, pointing in their direction. Jason took a second to figure out who I was pointing to.

"They're doctors. They work together at that practice over on Market Street; we fill a lot of prescriptions for their patients."

The funeral director ushered Tasha to the chair closest to the coffin. I scrutinized every detail of her appearance. She wore an appropriately subdued black dress and pearl earrings, and her hair smoothed back into a knot at the nape of her neck. Her eyes darted around the crowd as though hoping to find someone else to take the seat of honor. Finding no one, she perched on the edge of the chair, her lips pressed into a grim line.

She avoided looking at the casket entirely, gazing down at her lap instead. Though she had dark circles under her eyes, her expression was one of anger rather than sadness or grief. The priest opened his prayer book from his spot at the head of the coffin and began the service.

A dark sedan pulled into the cemetery from the far side of the lot, parking several feet in front of the hearse. Detective Moody climbed out.

"Crap," I said under my breath. I debated flitting

away, riding the wind to safety. In The Otherworld that's exactly what I would do, but of course I didn't have that option here—not with an audience. I inhaled sharply and held my ground. If he was here to arrest me in front of all these people, then so be it.

Jason followed my gaze to locate the source of my agitation. He stiffened and squared off when he saw the police officer, pivoting his body to face him. Moody glanced at the mourners, then marched over to where the two of us stood watching. I felt Jason relax beside me when Moody addressed me instead of him.

"Gloating over your handiwork?" he asked me. Jason peered back and forth between the two of us, trying to work out his meaning.

"What are you implying?" I challenged, though I know exactly what he meant.

"They say killers often attend their victims' funerals. What other reason do you have to be here? According to you, you didn't even know him," he answered, staring directly into my eyes.

"I'm guessing the forensics haven't come back on my knife yet? Otherwise you'd know it wasn't me," I bit back.

He shifted his weight, looking uncomfortable for a second. "Your fingerprints are all over the back of the pharmacy."

I swallowed the impulse to go off on him. Of *course* my fingerprints were there; I'd told him the entire story when we were down at the station. I knew he was trying to get a rise out of me, but I was determined to stay calm. My victory would be denying him the satisfaction.

"It's not like that. She's here with me," Jason said.

"She came to support me. Walter was more than my boss; he was a close friend. I didn't want to come here alone."

Moody looked me up and down, staring at my hair, tattoos and casual attire. He glanced at clean-cut Jason, decked out in a suit and tie. "You're telling me the two of you are together?"

"We're friends," Jason said, grabbing my hand.

"Opposites attract, I guess," he shrugged. " I'd keep an eye on that friend of yours. She's trouble," he said as he walked off towards the gravesite.

My cheeks burned with embarrassment. "I'm not sure why you did that, but thanks," I said, avoiding Jason's eyes.

"That asshole kept me at the police station answering questions for *hours* the other day. It was exhausting. For a minute I thought he was here to drag me in again, but he seems pretty convinced that you're the killer. How did that happen?" he asked, stunned.

"I swear I didn't kill him. I was just trying to return a backpack I found."

"Never thought you did. I'm pretty good at reading people, so I trust my instincts on that." He took a step closer to me and ran his fingertips down the length of my arm.

"Thank you," I said, my voice sounding breathless and flirtier than I had intended. It meant more than I cared to admit that he believed me.

"This bag you found... was it black with lots of pockets?" I nodded in response.

"Yeah, that was Strum's. Do you still have it?" I shook my head.

"The police confiscated it."

Over at the gravesite they had just finished reciting the Lord's Prayer. Tasha fiddled with her handbag, looking more awkward than ever. The rest of the crowd wore appropriately grim expressions; nothing in their demeanor suggested anything suspicious. Ida wiped her eyes with her handkerchief. Emma, sitting in a chair behind her, leaned forward and spoke to her in soothing tones. Moody stood to the side, evidently waiting for the service to end.

"If you ask me, my money is on the daughter. Look at her! *I'm* grieving more than she is," Jason said.

"Are you grieving?"

"Yeah, grieving my lost job," he smirked.

Father Michael ended the service and the mourners began to disperse, returning to their cars as they lowered the casket into the ground. Emma walked across the grass towards us, her navy skirt fluttering in the breeze. She smiled as she approached, her eyes on Jason.

"There you are. I wondered where you had gotten to," she said, grinning up at him. "You're coming back to the Apple Dumpling, right?"

"Hmmm," he pressed his lips together as he stared off over her head. "I don't think I'm invited."

"I'm inviting you right now, silly."

"I guess I could make an appearance, as long as Sloan comes with me."

The cheery expression fell from Emma's face. "Sure... Sloan, you should come too."

"No, that's okay." I said, taking a step back in an attempt to extricate myself from the situation. Emma clearly had a crush on Jason, and I had no interest in getting in the middle. "I'm not dressed for the occasion," I said, glancing down at my jeans.

Emma raised her eyebrows, nodding her head in Jason's direction. "Come. Please," she said. Her pleading eyes left me little choice.

I sighed. The last thing I wanted was to spend more time around accusing eyes. "Fine, but I'm not staying for long."

a sign in the front window of the Apple Dumpling Café read 'closed for a private function.' Jason was waiting outside as I pulled up to the curb, slipping into a parking spot just as a silver SUV vacated it.

"You didn't have to wait for me," I said, wishing that he hadn't. I didn't understand what I'd done to deserve all this attention from him.

"Like I was going to face that crowd alone," he said with a grin. "Sweet ride."

"Thanks," I said, glancing back at the Mustang. He was right; she was a beauty.

The café was already crawling with people. The small dining room was packed with mourners, all still wearing their somber suits and dresses. Emma stood behind the counter, away from the crowd, just as I preferred to be. She waved us over when we entered.

I followed Jason as he carved a path through the throng. Though I kept my head down, I still felt the scrutiny of the crowd as we passed by. A few people even mumbled that I had some nerve showing up there. I took a big breath to relax my nerves once we had made through to the other side of the dining room.

"Thank god you're here. I don't think Ida expected this many people," Emma said. "The sandwiches are holding out, but we're almost out of shoofly pie. There won't be any left for customers later today, and you know how she is about her pies." She pulled on an apron and tied it around her waist. "Ida asked me to watch over the refreshments, but would you mind taking over for me so I can make a couple more?"

"Sure, no problem. We're happy to help," Jason volunteered for both of us.

"That's great, thank you!" She squeezed his forearm before turning and disappearing into the kitchen.

Jason helped an elderly man make a plate while I crouched down to search under the counter for extra napkins. When I stood again, Tasha was waiting on the other side of the counter.

"Are you Jason Briggs?" she asked, waving off the plate he offered her.

"Yes ma'am, that's me. Can I help you with something?"

"With Walter gone, it looks like the pharmacy is my responsibility. I plan to keep the place open until I decide what to do with it," she said succinctly. "I don't know your plans, but would you be willing to continue working there, at least for the short term?"

Jason raised his eyebrows, his surprised expression a mirror image of my own. Her abrupt, straightforward manner felt out of place at her own father's funeral reception. She wasn't even trying to play the part of a grieving child. Even up close, I still didn't see any signs of sadness or remorse. In fact, I couldn't read any emotion in her eyes at all.

"Um, well, let me first say that I'm sorry for your loss," Jason stuttered.

"But yes, I could do that. It would be great to have some money coming in while I look for a new job."

"I'll pay you the same as you've been getting. You might not need a new job if I can find a buyer, but I can't make any promises on that," she said, holding out her hand to shake. "I've been looking for the other clerk, too. Douglas Simmons, I believe? Do you know where I can find him?"

"Yeah, Doug was working the late shift. I haven't seen him since—um, since the pharmacy closed. We weren't friends outside of work."

"I've been calling his number, but he doesn't ever answer."

A woman with white hair came up behind her, leaning on a cane for support.

"Tasha, do you remember me? I'm Mrs. Haas; I was your fourth-grade teacher. I sure remember you! Clumsiest child I ever met, and totally in denial about it," she chuckled. "Thought you were a gymnast. To think!" she smiled, lost in the memory and failing to notice as Tasha's cheeks grew pink. "But you've grown out of that, I can see. You've turned into a fine woman. I'm sorry about your father; such a pity."

"Mrs. Hass, I could *never* forget you," she said, turning abruptly and walking away without another word.

"Well! What was *that* all about?" the teacher asked,

looking at us with wide eyes. "She was never going to be an athlete, I'll tell you that much, but she was always such a quiet, polite little girl."

"Never mind her. What can we get for you to eat?" Jason asked. "Maybe some split pea soup? It was a bit chilly over at St. Francis today. This will warm you right up. Would you like me to carry it to your table for you?"

He ladled a steaming bowl full of soup and walked her to her seat. Emma came up beside me and watched them go.

"Look at that. He can even charm little old ladies," she said, eyeing him longingly. "Sloan, are you interested in him? Because I am, but I'd never be able to compete with someone like you."

"What do you mean, 'someone like me'?"

"Come on, you know you're gorgeous."

"So are you, Em. Really, But I'm not interested in the guy. He's all yours."

"Good," she said, her eyes lighting up as she scooted back to finish her pies.

Most of the people who came up to the counter didn't need assistance. We could easily have left our post, but I had no desire to mingle with the other guests. I passed the time by replenishing the drinks, napkins and anything else needed on the buffet, all the while waiting for the right moment to slip away without appearing rude to Ida or Jason.

Once it appeared that everyone who wanted food had gotten it, Ida rang the bell next to the cash register several times to quiet the chatter and get everyone's attention.

"We're here today to remember Walter Strum, our

neighbor, friend and father." She gestured toward Tasha. "I first met Walter when he opened his pharmacy here in Findale some thirty years ago. Never met a nicer man. He was always willing to help on any community project, and he really cared about our town." Several heads nodded in agreement as she spoke.

"He also helped me get my diabetes medication for free," said a diminutive elderly man from a table near the door. "I wouldn't be alive today if it weren't for him. He was a hero."

Tasha had gone stiff, her chest barely moving even to breathe. I turned to say something to Jason, but he had disappeared. I popped my head around the corner to see if he was with Emma.

"He snuck out the back door," she said, catching my gaze.

Great; he drags me here and then leaves without a word.

"...and never missed a Sunday mass." Father Michael was speaking when I turned back around. "He always volunteered to work bingo, and my goodness! What a family man. He never stopped talking about how proud—"

"Oh my god, SHUT UP!" Tasha screeched, her anger bursting through her veil of calm. "Family man? You have no idea what you're talking about. None of you do. He was a mean, cruel monster. I was never clumsy, *Mrs. Haas*. Those bruises and broken bones weren't from gymnastics. He beat my mother and me relentlessly, and when I tried to approach you for help, you brushed me off. You stupid, delusional people were willing to believe anything he told you because it was easier than believing the truth."

A hush fell over the café. Ida took a hesitant step in her direction. "Tasha, I'm so sorry. Truly, I didn't know."

"You didn't *want* to know. None of you did."

People hastened to get out of her way as Tasha stomped out of the café, slamming the door behind her hard enough to rattle the windows.

CHAPTER 10

I rolled pale yellow paint onto the wall, concentrating on the top half while Cormac painted the bottom. We overlapped each other's strokes, careful not to leave a line.

"It was quite a scene," I said as I stepped back to admire our handiwork. The fresh coat of paint had near miraculous results in renewing the look of the drywall.

"Aye, sounds like it. Poor lass, terrorized by someone who should have been her protector." Cormac dipped his roller in the paint tray.

"It would certainly explain why she didn't come back to help him after he had the stroke," I said, passing my roller over a spot on the wall that was not quite completely covered. "Everyone assumed she was a horrible daughter when all along, *he* was the horrible one."

Padraig ran by, enjoying the emptiness of the showroom. We had cleared out all the furniture in preparation for refurbishing the floor. He teased Max, holding one of his squeeze toys above his head. The little dog followed at his heels, leaping every few steps to try to grab it.

"Watch your step," I warned as Padraig came running in our direction, his eyes on the dog rather than on where he was going. He whipped his head around, but he didn't react fast enough to avoid clipping my paint tray with his foot. He leapt to avoid the paint sloshing over the side and landed on top of one of the long narrow light fixtures hanging from the fourteen-foot ceiling.

"So the boy can jump," I said, staring up at him.

"Aye, an ability inherited from his father. He's still working on controlling it." Cormac shook his head, looking up at his nephew with amusement.

"How does he get down once he gets himself up there?" I asked.

"I'm afraid that's a skill he has yet to master. I'm trying to teach him the art of rolling on his landing, but so far he's been too frightened to try it from so far up."

I went to get a rag to mop up the spilled paint, leaving Cormac to handle rescuing Padraig. Luckily the drop cloths had protected the wood floors. I came back into the showroom to find Cormac climbing up a chair he had placed underneath the boy. Padraig jumped off the light and into his uncle's arms. He looked no worse for wear when his uncle set him down. He picked up Max's squeaky toy and started running again.

"Padraig, go outside to play. You can take Max with you, just stay inside the fence on the side of the building," I said, eager to avoid another accident.

"Okay," he said, changing his trajectory without missing a beat. Max, still focused on the toy, followed right behind.

"Don't wander off," Cormac warned as we watched him leave the shop, slamming the door closed behind him.

"What did you find out from your visit to Montclair?" I asked, dipping my roller into the tray. I moved over to start on the back wall, the last one that needed to be painted.

"She's married, has two kids, lives in a big house—" The ringing of the chime over the entrance interrupted his story.

"There's a child outside running wild and bothering that dog of yours," said Ida, her indignation evident in her voice as she burst into the showroom. "Oh," she said, stopping short as she noticed the changes to the decor. "You're finally sprucing things up. It looks good so far! What's next? New floors?"

"Of course not; these are original to the building. We're going to refurbish them," I said, perhaps a bit sharply. The idea of replacing the beautiful wood offended me. "And I would hardly say the boy's running wild. He's in a fenced-in yard, after all."

"Oh, so he belongs to you too?" Ida replied, her eyebrows flying up in surprise.

"Actually, he belongs to me," said Cormac. He set down his roller and approached her.

Ida gasped and placed her hand to her chest, startled. "Oh my, I'm sorry. I didn't see you there."

"Please, do not apologize. My name is Cormac. What might your name be, lovely lady?"

"Oh, well—Ida. You can call me Ida." She appeared to be thrown off by his chivalrous demeanor. "You're a relative of Mr. Gobban's?" she asked, her voice a full octave higher than usual.

"Not every Little Person is related," I interjected, amused by her assumption.

"I know that!" she shot back. "It just seemed kind of coincidental that he's here at Gobban's old place. And to be honest, there's something about him that reminds me of your old friend."

"Don't fret, dear lady. Gobban was a valued friend. I would have been honored if he had been family, but alas, he was not. We do come from the same hometown, however."

"Hmm," said Ida as she gave me a smug look.

What she didn't know was that being from the same hometown was a euphemism for being the same type of fae. I studied Cormac's features. He didn't really resemble Gobban, but now I had to wonder: was there something about the Leprechauns' glamour that made them all appear related to humans? I had no way of knowing for sure, but perhaps this familiarity could work to our advantage. It could be pragmatic to claim relations in the future.

Ida inspected the wall Cormac had just finished painting. "You missed a spot," she said before turning back to face us. "Anyway, Sloan, I didn't see you this morning when you stopped by for breakfast. I wanted to thank you for jumping in at Walter's reception yesterday. Emma said you were a big help."

"You're welcome. I was happy to do it."

"Can you believe his daughter almost ruined the whole thing with all those terrible things she said?" She shook her head. "I couldn't believe she was making those accusations, speaking so poorly of the dead in front of all those people."

Here was the real purpose of Ida's visit, I thought: to gossip.

"You don't think Tasha's story was true?" I asked, surprised. She had seemed to believe her at first.

"I most certainly do not!" Ida boomed. "Walter Strum was a fine man. Everybody in this town knew it."

"I'm not sure I understand. Are you saying that she was lying about the broken bones and bruises?" While I wasn't a truthteller, able to hear the truth or a lie in another's voice as some fae could, Tasha's emotional outburst had sounded genuine to me.

"It was common knowledge that she took gymnastics classes but wasn't very good at it. She was constantly hurting herself, falling off the bars and such. Her mother even told me as much." Ida nodded her head, her words ringing with confidence.

"And what reason would this woman have to disparage her father in this way if it weren't true?" Cormac asked as he picked up his roller and touched up the spot she had pointed out.

Ida shrugged. "I really don't know, but her mother was one of my closest friends. She would have told me if that kind of thing had been going on. I'm sure of it. Even if she hadn't, I would have been able to tell. Patty wouldn't have stayed with a man like that—she was a very proud woman."

I smiled and let the conversation drop. I couldn't help but wonder if Patty's pride had been what kept her from admitting what was happening in her home. Perhaps she had been afraid of the man, or ashamed. Ida's confidence that her friend would have spoken up defied logic; there were so many reasons she might have stayed quiet.

"You know, I'm beginning to think that Tasha was the one who killed him. Best keep your distance from her," Ida warned.

"Tasha clearly didn't like her father, but she's been estranged from him for what—ten, maybe fifteen years? Why kill him now?" I asked, not buying it.

"Well," started Ida, her voice taking on a conspiratorial tone. "Evelyn told me that Gladys told her that Walter had a big life insurance policy. And she should know, her husband was the one who sold it to him years ago. Tasha is still listed as the primary beneficiary. She killed him for the money, that's what I say."

The chimes rang again and in strode Tommy, interrupting the conversation inside. He was once again in his navy-blue police uniform, clearly back on duty. He had Max tucked under an arm, his other hand holding a fistful of Padraig's collar.

"I found these two running wild outside," he said, letting Max down and releasing the boy's shirt. "Shouldn't he be in school? And Sloan, really? How many times do I have to tell you: when you're in town, you have to keep your dog on a leash."

I frowned, exchanging a glance with Cormac. Tommy wouldn't mistake the fenced-in yard for running wild the way Ida had. ""He wasn't in the yard?" I asked, confused.

"Not hardly," said Tommy. "I found him wandering up and down the street, peeking through car windows. If he were any older I might have taken him for a car thief."

"I'm sorry. It won't happen again, will it, Padraig?"

The kid was standing forlornly to the side, shoulders slumped, head bowed and working hard to keep his gaze glued to the floor.

"What about school? Is he ditching?" Tommy put his hands on his hips as he eyed the little Leprechaun.

"What, are you the truancy police now?" asked Ida. I threw her a warning glance. The last thing I needed right now was to antagonize anyone on the police force.

"I teach my nephew myself," Cormac, an icy edge to his voice, insulted at a perceived slight of the care he gave his nephew. "He needs no one else."

Tommy looked at the indignant Leprechaun, raising his eyebrows in surprise. *Great! Another one wanting to give the police a hard time.*

Tommy grabbed a notepad and pen from his pocket, looking none too happy. "You said you're homeschooling him? Have you registered with the state? It's required."

"They just arrived in town, Tommy. We'll get every-thing situated in the next day or two," I interjected, not wanting the situation to blow up. "I apologize if Padraig was bothering other people's cars. We'll give him a talking to."

Tommy relaxed his shoulders and put his notepad away. "Okay, that's fine. I'll give you this: the kid has an active imagination. He said something about there being no cars in The Otherworld—as if another world really existed," he laughed.

"Yes, a great imagination," I said, covering my alarm with an awkward smile. Padraig had talked about Faery to a human! If he didn't learn to be more careful, he was going to get us all exposed.

"Well I must say, I would think you'd have more

important things to worry about than a rambunctious child and his dog," Ida huffed.

Tommy's head turned. "Excuse me?"

"Are you here playing truancy officer? No, you're here to arrest Sloan, aren't you? I'm telling you, you're barking up the wrong tree. It was the daughter, I'm sure of it. You're wasting your time here when you should be out tailing her."

Tommy let out an exasperated breath. "No, Ida, I haven't come to arrest Sloan, but that really isn't any of your business. I do need to speak with her though, if you don't mind. I'll take your advice on how to do my job under advisement."

The older woman pressed her lips together and pouted. "Well, Miss Sloan, I came here for a reason too. Now that the dishwasher is working beautifully, one of the fridges has gone on the fritz. Will you come by and take a look at it?"

I nodded. "Sure, but not until tomorrow." I didn't what to lose our momentum on the shop renovations.

"That will be fine, thank you," said Ida, "And good day to you, *Officer Lynch*," she said, marching past him and out of the store with her head held high. I sighed.

"Tommy, what did you need? Something I can fix for you?" I asked, not really believing he had come in for my services.

He shuffled his feet and looked off into the distance. Clearly, he wasn't here to give me good news.

"Is there somewhere we can talk?" he asked me, glancing sidelong at Cormac. The Leprechaun had resumed painting the back wall. I led the officer towards my desk on the opposite side of the showroom, knowing full well that Cormac would still be able to hear whatever he said.

"I'm listening," I told him.

"Sloan, I think it's time for you to get a lawyer."

"What? Why? There's no way my blade could have matched the one that made the wounds. What more does Moody need before he admits he's wrong about me?"

Tommy shifted his weight, clearly uncomfortable. "I'm not supposed to tell you this, but evidently your knife disappeared before they could test it. Everyone's pointing fingers at everyone else, but the bottom line is that it's gone."

"Oh," I said, closing my eyes for a second as I processed this new information. I had known the spear-head would disappear eventually, but I'd hoped it would stay at least long enough to clear my name. It was supposed to be on my side, after all. "So the next time you come here, you really might be here to arrest me."

"I hope not," Tommy replied, "but you should be prepared."

CHAPTER 11

*O*nce we had finished painting the main showroom, I left the shop in search of food and returned twenty minutes later with our lunch. Max greeted me in his usual fashion as I walked through the door, his tail wagging his entire body. I leaned over, balancing our food precariously in one hand so that I could scratch his head. Voices floated to me from the workroom in the back of the store.

"Padraig, we have gone over this too many times already. Fae law dictates that while we're in the Human World, you must never do or say anything to let them know that you're a Leprechaun. That includes talking about The Otherworld. If you don't learn to be more careful, I will have no choice but to take you back to Faery. Do you understand?"

"Yes, sir." The boy's voice quivered as he fought to keep tears in check. His distress was heartbreaking. I hurried into the room to put an end to the scolding, although it was well deserved.

"Lunch is here!" I said, placing a flat square box on the worktable and a stack of paper plates next to it. Padraig lifted the lid to peek inside.

"What is it?"

"Only the best thing humans have ever invented," I teased, flipping the box open. "Pizza!"

I lifted out the first slice, tendrils of cheese stretching long as I pulled it away from the rest of the pie. I used two fingers to break the connections and placed the slice on a plate in front of Padraig, repeating the process for Cormac and myself. Padraig eyed his slice suspiciously.

"How do you eat it?"

I picked up my pizza, folded it in half longways and bit off the tip. He followed my lead, his face lighting up as he chewed.

"Man, this *is* good."

Cormac watched us both with a grin before starting in on his lunch.

"Tell me more about your trip to Montclair. You were saying that Tasha had a family before Ida interrupted you?" I prompted. "Do you think she needs the insurance money?"

He shrugged a shoulder. "She lives in a big house. Her husband is a stockbroker, and she works for a group of attorneys. Their children go to a private school."

"It sounds like they're well off, but looks can be deceiving," I said as I handed Padraig a paper napkin to wipe the sauce from his chin.

"Quite right. Rumor has it that her husband is sickly and has been out of work for a while."

"Did you see any sign of a red pickup truck?"

"Not in that neighborhood," he chuckled.

"What's a school?" Padraig asked, picking up a piece of pepperoni and popping it into his mouth.

"It's a place where humans send their children to learn their lessons," Cormac answered. Padraig's eyes grew wide. "You will be educated by your family, just as your father and I were. It is the way of our people."

"This school though, it's full of other children? And I could go there?"

"No. They don't teach the skills to be a proper tradesman there. Skills we Leprechauns have passed down through generations."

"It isn't a place to go play all day," I interjected to soften Cormac's refusal. "You have to study hard. There are teachers there, adults who you have to listen to. They give you what they call 'homework,' lessons you need to complete after school."

"Please, Uncle Cormac? Please can I go?" Padraig begged, undeterred by my description. "You could still teach me those other things when I come home!"

"You spoke of Faery to the first stranger you encountered. The only thing worse would have been dropping your glamour. How can we trust you to keep our secrets day after day around hundreds of them?" Padraig continued to look up at him, pleading with his eyes. "There can be no moving at super speed or any other Leprechaun tricks," Cormac warned. The boy bobbed his head up and down. "And you must hide that many things are new to you."

"I can do it! I promise I can." Cormac still looked skeptical.

"He hasn't acclimated to living here, that's true, but maybe being immersed in his new world would help speed things up," I offered, not sure why I was encouraging the boy. "You could allow it on a tentative basis to see how he does. An experiment, so to speak."

"I'll think about it," Cormac said. Padraig's face lit up; clearly, he took his uncle's response as a step closer to yes. "But for now, we must get back to work."

*B*esides the large showroom, the store had several smaller rooms. We planned to leave the workshop as is, other than Cormac rearranging things to suit his needs for his craft. Cormac wanted to use one room for giving music lessons, so we made sure to include it in the renovations.

The third room, located behind the corner I had been using for my shop, housed shelves that now held the broken appliances that had cluttered the shop. My Leprechaun friend had insisted that they be out of sight.

We had bought four-foot-tall maple cabinets that would complement the refurbished floorboards. We planned to use them to create a wall that, together with the checkout counter already in place, would mark the perimeter of my shop within a shop. I was excited to have an attractive space to call my own, but we still had work to do before making it a reality—like assembling the cabinets.

We began by laying out all the components, organizing them by putting like pieces with like pieces. I put Padraig in charge of the multiple piles of screws to keep him occupied, instructing him when to hand us them and which ones we needed. Instructions in hand, I got comfortable on the floor.

"Wait, these floorboards are already sanded," I said, wondering why I hadn't noticed it earlier. I ran my fingers over the smooth surface, enjoying the natural energy that radiated from it. "What did you do, stay up all night working on them?"

"They were sanded last night, but not by me," Cormac spoke without lifting his eyes from his task. He assembled one of the cabinets with ease, barely even peeking at the instructions.

"You left a stranger alone in the shop overnight?" I asked. It struck me odd for Cormac to take such a risk.

"I didn't let him in; he's been here all along," said Cormac, smiling as footsteps clomped down the stairway from the apartment on the second floor. "That must be him."

I stood to face the door, wondering who could have been hanging around without my knowledge. Certainly they had to be fae, not human.

The man who entered the showroom was a stranger to me, but recognizable right away as a Brounie. He was short, but not as short as a Leprechaun. His ears had elongated points on the ends and his hair was wiry and coarse.

"What do I smell?" he asked, crinkling his nose.

"Pizza!" Padraig proclaimed happily.

"You bought pizza? Why would you ever do that? I could have made you one a thousand times better than anything you could find around here."

"I bought it. There's a couple of slices left if you want one," I offered, just to see his reaction. His face contorted into an expression of disgust.

"Oh, it's you," he said, fumbling his words when he

recognized who had spoken to him. He rushed toward me, reaching out with his hand. "Hello. I'm Michan, and you are the famous *Bláth Dorcha.*"

"Please, call me Sloan here in the Human World," I said, pasting a fake smile on my face. I had hoped to have left the fame and notoriety attached to that name back in Faery.

His face flushed. "Aye, of course. I should know better."

Max inspected the newcomer by sniffing around the Brounie's pant leg. Michan wrinkled his brow. He looked so uncomfortable that I picked up the cocker spaniel and held him for the rest of the conversation.

"Michan has been keeping the apartment upstairs in good order. Not a speck of dust in the place. You would never have known it had stood empty for so long," Cormac said. "He's also been taking care of the store and that thing you call a home."

"You've been here all this time?" I asked. Brounies were creatures of the night, taking care of the homes and people around them without looking for recompense. As a matter of fact, they took it as a huge insult if you tried to give them anything to show your gratitude, so much so that they often left to find another household to care for if you made the mistake of expressing your appreciation beyond a simple thank you. My face flushed with embarrassment as I thought about the many little clues I'd overlooked that pointed to a Brounie's presence.

"I tried to cook for you as well, but this tiny beast kept eating whatever I set out for you," he said, shooting Max a disparaging look.

"Did you come here with Gobban?" I asked.

"Nay, I came with you. Like many, I'm grateful for your part in the final Unseelie war. It is an honor to serve you."

"You have more supporters in Faery than you know," Cormac agreed.

My mouth dropped open as they spoke. Clearly, they both were nuts. My notoriety in The Otherworld hadn't been a pleasant experience, especially with my fellow Sidhe. The majority of them were suspicious of me for being born Unseelie, and they looked down on anyone vile enough to tattoo their skin. I kept these thoughts to myself.

"But why not show yourself?" I asked.

"It isn't our way. We stay in the shadows until we're invited to come out."

So you can't tell anyone you're around until they invite you to, but they don't know you're there to make the invitation. Kind of stupid if you ask me.

"Well, you must come out of hiding now," I said, smiling to hide my snarky musings. "You did a great job on the floor." He stretched an inch taller than his five feet with pride.

"Cormac, I trust the floors are to your satisfaction as well. When do I collect my instrument?"

"Aye, my best guitar, as we agreed. You can have it tomorrow after you've completed the job. The floors still need varnish. In the meantime, perhaps you wouldn't mind helping Sloan finish the cabinets? I must be off. Padraig and I need to get to the school before it closes so that I can enroll my nephew."

CHAPTER 12

It was after two by the time I walked through the rear door of the Apple Dumpling Café the next afternoon. I found Emma alone in the kitchen, aggressively scrubbing the grill with both hands. A film of perspiration covered her face, her expression grim.

She jumped and stepped back as I entered, wiping an arm across her forehead. "You startled me!" she said, smiling. "I guess I was in my own little world."

"Are you here by yourself?" I asked, wondering why it was so quiet.

"Gretchen's cleaning the dining room. It's been such a slow day. We're hoping to get everything done early so we can slip out right at closing." The café only served breakfast and lunch, closing each day at three o'clock. She shook out her right hand, cradling it with her left and massaging it as she spoke.

"Is Ida here?" I asked. "She ordered me over to fix one of the refrigerators."

"She told me you were coming," Emma nodded. "She

had to run, but she left you a slice of shoofly pie." She gestured to the stainless-steel worktable on the other side of the kitchen where a ceramic plate with a large piece of pie sat waiting for me. I grinned; it was hard to stay angry at the woman.

Emma nodded her approval as I grabbed a coffee mug and strode out to the dining room. Gretchen had her back to me as she swept the floor, earphones stuffed in her ears and completely oblivious to my presence. I drained the last of the pot of coffee into my cup, filling it three quarters full and topping it off with cream. I slipped back into the kitchen with a twinge of guilt, knowing that Gretchen would have to brew a fresh pot if any last-minute customers arrived.

"Want to share the pie with me?" I asked Emma as I took a big gulp of coffee.

"Well, maybe a bite or two," she said, snatching up a second fork.

I pulled up two stools that Ida kept tucked away on the far side of the pantry, placing the first on one side of the table for Emma and making myself comfortable opposite her. I dug into the pie with enthusiasm, savoring the sweet taste of molasses in each bite. Emma took a little more time to pick up her fork, her expression drawn and pinched.

I examined her more closely, noticing for the first time how thin she had grown. Her face was pale and shiny with sweat. Her strawberry blond hair, usually tucked neatly under her hairnet, was a mass of tangles.

"Are you okay, Em? You don't look well." Tears glistened in her eyes.

"Every muscle in my body aches, and my wrist is

killing me. I can barely use it without wanting to scream."

"From the fall? After all this time?" I asked, incredulous. Then again, perhaps humans take longer to heal than the fae.

"The problem is that I ran out of my pain medication, and the pharmacy has been closed since Mr. Strum was —um—died. I don't know how to get it refilled." A large tear rolled down her cheek.

"Who told you they were closed?" I asked, taking another generous forkful of the pie.

"Jason."

"That must have been before Tasha asked him to come back to work. It was open when I drove past it on my way here."

Emma's eyes widened and darted around manically. "I gotta go, I've got to get over there."

"Whoa," I said, glancing at a clock on the wall. "You only have half an hour left until the café closes; you don't want to leave Gretchen here on her own. Let me fix the refrigerator, then I'll drive you," I insisted, not wanting her to drive herself there in this agitated state.

She took a deep, calming breath. "Okay, you're right, it's just a few more minutes. Thank you. It's that fridge over there," she said, pointing. "Heat was radiating from the back of it, so we turned it off before it could break down altogether."

I nodded. I had expected this refrigerator to be the culprit. It was old and had given Ida trouble a couple of months earlier.

"I told her she needs to clean behind this one more often, now that it's getting older," I grumbled as I walked over to it. I pulled the appliance away from the wall, letting loose a cloud of dust and dirt onto Emma's clean floor.

*T*he atmosphere inside the pharmacy was understandably different than the last time I had been there. I was relieved to find that it no longer smelled of blood and death. The store was brightly lit and busy with customers browsing the aisles and lining up at the register. Music played softly in the background.

I held the door open, hesitant to enter. It had just occurred to me that it might not be appropriate for me to be there, considering the suspicion I was under. Emma pushed past me and made a beeline to the drop-off counter. She tapped her fingernails on the countertop impatiently while she waited for Jason to finish helping the customers at the checkout counter.

I threw back my shoulders and stepped into the store. I had done nothing wrong, no matter what Detective Moody might think. If anyone had a problem with me being here—well, tough.

I browsed the aisles to entertain myself while I waited for Emma and soon found myself facing the shelves of soda. I grabbed a six-pack of cola with a grin, imagining how much fun it would be to introduce Padraig to this new delicacy. I carried it up to the register and checked in on Emma.

Her rhythmic tapping on the counter had stopped, but she was pacing back and forth in front of the drop off window. I glanced in the opposite direction at the business office and saw Tasha sitting at a desk piled high with folders, books, and ledgers. She looked up at me and I jumped like a kid getting caught with their hand in the cookie jar.

It suddenly occurred to me how incredibly long it was taking Jason to ring up the handful of items for the customer in front of me. I peered over the gentleman's shoulder and saw him tallying up the customer's bill with pen and paper, something I had never seen in a retail establishment.

He painstakingly calculated the man's change and pulled it out of the open cash drawer. The man snatched his bag, took the change and handwritten receipt and stomped off, shaking his head.

"Jason," Emma hissed in a stage whisper as I approached the register.

"You better go help her first or she might explode," I said, chuckling as I set down my soda. I tried not to eavesdrop on their conversation, but they were too close. Even though they spoke in hushed voices, it was impossible for me not to hear them.

"Jason, why didn't you tell me the pharmacy was open again? I ran out of my medicine two days ago."

"Come on, Emma, I did tell you. I also told you that I can't fill the prescription. I'm not a pharmacist; we need someone licensed to check my fills." Emma looked furious. Jason held up a hand to cut her off before she could start to argue with him.

"Tasha hired one on a part-time basis. He'll be coming in every night to look over what I've done, starting tonight. You'll be able to pick up your refill tomorrow. Have you tried asking Dr. Greenwood if he has any samples he can give you in the meantime?"

I really had no business hearing this. I wandered around the counter to look at the register to distract myself, curious to know why Jason hadn't been using it. It was an antique cash register straight from the 60's with a beige metal case and cream and green colored buttons. Some people would even classify it as a collectible. Several of the buttons looked stuck. I tried to lift them with a fingertip, but they held fast.

"I'm sorry about the wait. We really should have a second clerk during the busy times," Tasha commented from over my shoulder.

"Oh, no, I'm sorry, I shouldn't be back here. So I guess you never located that guy, um, Douglas Simmons? The guy who was working with Jason before... all this?" I struggled with how to word my question, cringing inwardly at what came out.

"No. He still isn't answering his phone and he hasn't returned my messages, which seems weird to me. Aren't all these millennials supposed to be glued to their phones? I guess he just doesn't want the job."

I didn't know what to say to that, so I hastily changed the subject. "I noticed the register isn't working, and fixing things is what I do. I could get it running again if you want."

"That thing has been here since I was a kid. I'm going to trash it as soon as I get around to ordering a new one. This place will never sell with that old thing."

I gritted my teeth, trying not to show my aggravation. This was a beautiful machine. A treasure, not a piece of junk.

"How about I make you a deal? I'll fix it so Jason can

use it until the new one arrives. When it does, you give this baby to me instead of junking it."

Tasha shrugged. "Sounds like a win-win. Can you come back when the store is closed?"

"No problem at all. I'm a bit of a night owl anyway," I told her. I felt a twinge of guilt as I spoke to her. "I'm Sloan, by the way. I guess to be fair I should tell you that half of the town thinks I killed your father."

"I know who you are, and don't worry about it. The other half thinks I did it."

"Jason, come on! Don't do this to me," Emma said, her voice rising to a whine. Her cheeks flushed when she saw Tasha and me staring at her.

Jason angled his body away from us and whispered, "Okay, okay. Just remember, I could get in serious trouble for this so don't tell anyone. As far as anyone else is concerned, a refill had been sitting here since before Walter passed."

No one else at this distance would have been able to hear him, but my fae senses made it almost impossible not to. Besides, Emma had said that she needed this medication. I sure wasn't going to interfere.

"Here, let me check you out," Tasha said, noticing the soda on the counter.

"You know what, I'll wait for my friend," I said, grabbing the cola and stepping to the side. Tasha helped the new customer faster and more efficiently than Jason, then returned to the desk in the office.

"Everything okay?" I asked as Emma joined me. She smiled sweetly.

"Perfect. He found my prescription; Walter must

have already filled it. Isn't that wonderful?" she said, lying without blinking an eye.

Jason came up to the register and laid a small white prescription bag on the counter. I put my soda down next to it.

"I'm sorry I got so cross, Jason. Let me make it up to you?" Emma smiled up at him, tossing her strawberry blonde hair over her shoulder. "How about we meet for drinks at JR's tonight, say around seven? First round's on me."

"Sure, I can always go for a plate of their fries. How about you, Sloan? Want to join us?"

Emma's chest deflated, her exuberance evaporating.

I stared at him, wide-eyed in astonishment. Could this guy really be that stupid?

"No, you two go. I have to fix this cash register."

"Come on, that can wait," said Jason, glancing at Tasha.

I wanted to slap the guy. Why wasn't he getting it? This was the second time he'd put me in an awkward situation. This time, I wasn't having it. "No, I don't think I can."

"Sloan, you should totally join us," Emma replied, a lackluster grin plastered across her sullen face.

"Okay, well... Emma, why don't you go get a bottle of water so you can take your medication right away?" I suggested. Jason and I watched her walk away. When I was sure she was out of earshot, I turned on him. "You're an idiot."

"What? What do you mean?"

"She asked you out on a date and you invited me along," I seethed.

"It's not like that, We're just friends."

"Really? Have you told her that? She obviously has a thing for you," I snapped. He had managed to miss what anyone else would find obvious.

"Well I'm sorry but I don't feel the same way, and now I need you to come out with us more than ever. I don't want her getting the wrong idea."

I shook my head, glaring at him. "No. I'm not playing games. Emma's my friend. If you want to be my friend, you have to be honest and have a conversation with her."

"Okay, fine. I promise. If I speak to her, will you come out with us?"

"Just make sure you do it."

CHAPTER 13

I plopped onto my bed and covered my eyes with my forearm, grateful to be home after a long day. I groaned as I remembered that it wasn't over yet. How did I get myself in this situation? I would have simply not shown up for the rendezvous at JR's, but Emma had been afraid that Jason wouldn't show if I didn't come. She had made me promise to be there.

I felt a soft thump on the bed, followed a moment later by wet kisses on my cheek. *Count on this little guy to boost my spirits*, I thought, pulling myself up to lean against my headboard. Max eagerly climbed into my lap. I brushed his fur out of his eyes.

"You need a haircut, little man." He wagged his tail as if excited by the prospect. If only he'd known what I had suggested! He wasn't fond of his regular trips to the groomer. I grinned; Max could cheer up even the most miserable person.

He rolled off my lap and lay on his back alongside my leg. I rubbed his belly as I thought about Tasha in her designer suit, her head bent over volumes of old-fashioned ledgers. Would this sophisticated, highly educated woman really have come home to kill her father because her bank account was getting low? It seemed unlikely.

I realized that I believed her story: that Walter had abused her as a child. Most people have trouble imagining a person hurting their offspring; it goes so horribly against nature. I knew better. My grandfather had tried to kill me in my infancy. I had been luckier than Tasha. My adoptive father treated me with nothing but love until the day he passed away.

If I had been in Tasha's place, would I have wanted my torturer dead? Maybe.

I gave Max a pat and got up, looking for something else to fill my mind. My new flute caught my eye. I examined it in the light of the fading sun that filtered through the bedroom window. The intricate design carved into the wooden instrument was breathtaking.

I held it to my lips and blew gently, moving my fingers up and down over the body to play a scale. The tone was round and pure; it was a magnificent flute. Next I played a rollicking jig Cormac had taught me, surprised that I remembered it after a break of months.

Max jumped to his feet and howled, not at all impressed with my efforts.

"Hey! It's not *that* bad," I said with a chuckle. Actually, I thought I was pretty good. I placed the flute back in its case and flipped the clasps closed. "I guess I can't delay it any longer. Time to take my shower."

· · ·

*J*R's Pub and Restaurant on Main Street was a popular night spot with both locals and tourists. We were in the off-season between summer and the fall foliage, and the number of visitors to the Poconos was down. The sparse number of patrons in the restaurant reflected that fact.

Jason sat at the bar nursing a beer. He wore a muted green button-down shirt that nicely complemented his hazel eyes. It was easy to see why Emma had fallen for him; you couldn't fault the guy's looks.

I thought of the promise he'd made me to have an honest conversation with Emma. Since she didn't appear to have arrived yet, now would be the perfect time to ask him about it.

"Can I get you a table?" the hostess asked.

"No thanks, I'm meeting a friend at the bar." She nodded and smiled, turning to ask the same question of a couple who came in behind me.

A short, muscular man came up and leaned on the bar next to Jason. The newcomer seemed to know him and started up a conversation. I stayed put and listened with unabashed curiosity.

"So I hear the old crank is dead," Muscles said, a tinge of amusement in his voice. He signaled the bartender for a beer. "Couldn't have happened to a better guy."

"Nice," Jason said derisively, frowning up at him. "Don't you have any respect? The man was murdered."

"He was insane! His rules were insane, and his temper was insane." The bartender placed a mug of pale

ale in front of him. "Someone told me he started filling Larry's prescriptions after I left," he said, taking a swig. "What changed? I didn't think the bastard would ever change his mind."

Jason shrugged. "Needed the business, I guess."

"I don't get it. What happened? Did he start treating his customers as bad as he treated his employees? If so, I'm just surprised someone didn't kill'm sooner."

"Don't say things like that," Jason said, looking around nervously to see if anyone else had heard. "Next thing you know you'll have the police snooping around and asking questions."

The other man laughed as he turned to leave. "If I'm a suspect, so is every other idiot who worked for him. Every one of us hated the man, including you."

I waited until he walked away before joining Jason at the bar.

"Who was that?" I asked as he stood to greet me.

"Ed Parker." I waited for him to elaborate. When he didn't, I ventured another question.

"A friend of yours?"

"Not really. He was a clerk at the pharmacy before me. Walter fired him when he found out his girlfriend was pregnant. Babies out of wedlock went against one of his many rules." He offered me the stool next to his before returning to his seat. "What would you like to drink?"

"Does he drive a red pickup?"

"Come on, forget about him." He put up a finger to signal the bartender. "Now, tell me what you're drinking."

I let him order me a beer while my thoughts

continued to run on Ed Parker. I hadn't noticed him at the funeral, but that was hardly surprising considering the circumstances.

Could Ed have killed his old boss? He obviously hated the man, but would he be stupid enough to talk that horribly about Walter if he had killed him? And what about this Doug guy? How come no one could get ahold of him?

"—and after all that, she's decided to close the store early." Jason's disgruntled voice disrupted my thoughts. "What about the people who can't get there earlier? How are they supposed to get their meds?"

"Tasha cut the store's hours?" I asked, feeling like I came into the conversation late.

"Yeah. She's a nut job, totally obsessed with money. Walter didn't trust computers; everything in the store was done like it was the dark ages, like that stupid cash register that's been broken since the day I started." I nodded my head to show I was listening, though I wasn't sure why I was being subjected to this tirade. "She keeps mumbling 'where's the money' while combing through the receipts. And when she couldn't find a replacement for Doug, she said the place doesn't make enough money to keep the lights on after six."

"Oh. That's too bad," was all I could think of to say. "Emma is coming, isn't she?"

"Yeah, she said she was coming. I think you were wrong about her though—when I spoke to her earlier, she agreed we were just friends. She said she felt the same way."

I snorted. "Of course she did, what else could she say?" I had no doubt that I was right in making Jason set the record straight with Emma. At least this way he wasn't leading her on. I glanced at my watch: it was seven thirty. She should have been here half an hour ago.

"You're sure she said she'd be here?"

He pulled his phone out of his pocket. "I'll text her."

The bartender set a plate of french fries in front of us. Jason put his phone face down on the bar, picking up a long fry and dipping it in ketchup. He slid the plate closer to me.

"Have some. They're the best fries in town."

JR's had live music every night in the dining room. I sampled a fry as the night's entertainment, a local cover band, took the stage. The female lead singer's melodious voice was perfectly suited for the romantic Whitney Houston ballad cover they chose to start their set.

The loud music made conversation difficult. We enjoyed the next couple of songs in silence as we sipped our beers and munched on fries. When the dish was empty, Jason tapped me on my arm and gestured to the door. I followed him outside.

"Emma didn't answer my text. I'm going to give her a call, but it was too noisy in there."

I strolled up the street to where my Mustang was parked as he made the call, leaning my butt against the front fender. Jason walked toward me a moment later, holding his phone away from his ear.

"She didn't pick up. Maybe I did make her angry. Why don't you try?"

"I don't have a cellphone."

"Really? Not even a flip phone?"

"Nope. You might as well know now, I'm an old gadget kind of girl."

"A flip phone *is* an old gadget," he said with a laugh.

"*H*ey, how about letting me take this beauty for a spin?" he asked, running his fingers along the top edge of the Mustang's fender. "What year is it, a '67?"

"It's a '68 and no, you can't drive it." I stuffed my hands into my jeans pockets, jamming my car keys further down.

"You sure? There's this beautiful spot in the mountains that overlooks the entire valley. On a night like this the stars shine brighter there than anywhere else you've ever stargazed. Let me take you there. You won't regret it, it's breathtaking." He moved closer to me as he spoke, his physical proximity as hypnotic as his words. I turned away to break the spell.

"Which one is your car?" I asked, glancing at the vehicles parked on either side of the street.

"Believe it or not, I'm still driving my Mom's 2003 Mitsubishi. Not a classic, like this beauty. It's old and it spends most of its time in the shop. It's over at Burt's Auto right now, and to be honest, I don't have the money to fix it." He frowned and looked away, seemingly embarrassed by his admission. "I Ubered here. If I keep doing that, I'll never be able to save money." He chuckled half-heartedly.

I held my breath, worried he was going to ask me to do the repairs. I had an agreement with Burt: I stayed away from cars and he sent all other mechanical repairs my way.

"You're not really going to deny me the chance to take this baby for a ride, are you?"

"Do you even know how to drive stick?" I asked, my resistance weakening. He grinned, sensing my attitude change.

"As a matter fact, I do." He held out his hand for the keys. I stared at him, still debating whether or not I was okay with this. Sighing, I pulled the keys out of my pocket.

"You better treat her right. You strip her gears and I'll kick your ass." He laughed, which annoyed me. "I'm not joking. I can do it."

"I have no doubt," he said, placing his hand over his heart. "I promise to treat her with all the respect she so greatly deserves."

I relinquished the keys, comforting myself with the thought that if he messed with my car, I would simply hold *Dominion* over him. I would force him to pull over and let me drive, and no one would fault me for it.

Jason opened the passenger door for me, closing it firmly once I had settled into the seat. He skipped around to the driver's side and settled himself behind the steering wheel, starting the motor with a turn of the key. He flashed a grin. "Listen to that engine purr!"

He took a second to get acquainted with the controls, turning on the lights and adjusting the rear-view mirror.

"What happened to the shoulder strap?" he asked as he fastened the seatbelt across his lap.

"The '68 didn't have them, so take it easy."

I watched him closely as he released the emergency brake, stepped on the clutch and shifted into first gear.

He executed the next couple of shifts smoothly; apparently he really *could* drive stick.

As we drove out of town, I forced myself to let my balled-up, tension-filled fists unclench. I watched him for a while; he wore the car well. When I finally shifted my gaze from his handsome face to the road, I inhaled sharply in shock. We were half a mile from my home.

"Where exactly are we going?" I asked, eyeing him suspiciously. Did he know where I lived?

"We're almost there. Have patience," he smiled, leaning forward to turn on the radio. He drove past the trailer without giving it a second glance. I relaxed back into my seat.

"You said you come here often?" I asked as he turned down a road that looped around Pine Ridge Estates. How well could I be monitoring the property if people were coming and going without me noticing?

"I stumbled on this overlook about a month ago, and I've come here maybe six or seven times since then. We're almost there."

Jason drove up a steep hill that went along the back of the estate until he reached a stretch where the road leveled off. He pulled off onto a section of the shoulder that had been worn down by multiple cars parking in the same spot. Clearly, he wasn't the only one who'd been enjoying the scenery from here.

Though he had parked facing the view, we got out of the Mustang and met at the front of the car to give ourselves a better vantage point. He hadn't exaggerated the beauty of the vista before us. The stars and waxing crescent moon illuminated the buildings on the estate, all clustered together in the foreground. Further out, the town of Findale glittered. The streetlights glowed against the dark sky.

"Isn't it magnificent? It's pretty during the day, too, but it's nothing compared to this," Jason said, his voice hushed in reverence. He reached out and took my hand.

The reflection of the stars in his eyes made him even more attractive, but something held me back from encouraging his attention. Something other than my friend calling dibs on him, although of course that should have been enough. I searched his face as I tried to understand my hesitancy, but I found no clues there.

"Look at that section there, that field out past the houses and before the woods," Jason instructed, pointing down at the estate. "It's weird—it's just a patch of wild-flowers, but there's something just so magical about it."

I took a step closer to the edge of the bluff to get a better view. It took me a moment to figure out which part of the estate he was pointing to, but then I had to grin. There was a good reason Jason found that area special; Pixies lived in that garden, invisible to humans unless their eyes had been opened to the fae. What he didn't understand was that their playful, youthful energy reached us even at this height.

"Don't get too close to the edge; I don't want to lose you," said Jason, pulling me back and wrapping his arms around me.

A breeze picked up, accentuating the soothing sounds of nature in the air. The chatter of the Pixies was intoxi-cating. He leaned down to kiss me and I had made up my mind to let him.

In the instant before our lips could meet, a new sound assaulted me. A horrifying wail pierced my ears, followed by heart wrenching sobs filled with horrendous pain and loss. I jerked away from him, spinning to face the town as tears sprang to my eyes. I blinked furiously to keep them in check. I suddenly felt sick to my stomach.

"Sloan, what's wrong?" Jason asked. I couldn't possibly explain to him that I'd heard a sound on the wind, something that he would never have been able to hear himself. There was no easy excuse I could give him for my mood shift, but neither could I shake it off and go back to flirting.

"We have to go," I said.

"Was it me? Did I do something wrong?" he asked, furrowing his brow as he recognized my distress. "Are you okay? You don't look well."

"I just need to get out of here."

CHAPTER 14

"*I*f I did something to offend you, I'm truly sorry," Jason said, watching me out of the corner of his eye as he drove us back to town.

"It's not that. I guess those fries didn't agree with my stomach," I said, knowing it was a lame excuse. I stared out the side window at the trees rushing past as we sped down the road.

The conversation waned, leaving the music on the radio to fill the silence for the rest of the ride. Jason pulled the Mustang into an empty parking space right across from JR's. I touched his arm as he put the car in neutral.

"Why don't you let me drop you off at your place?" I asked.

"That's okay, it's too early to call it a night. I think I'll listen to the music inside for a while." Jason came around and opened my door for me. "You should go home and get some sleep. I hope you feel better in the morning."

He leaned in to kiss my lips, but I turned to give him my cheek instead. He said goodnight with a fake smile glued to his face. A wave of guilt washed over me as I watched him disappear into JR's.

I couldn't decide what to do next. I desperately wanted to find the person whose agonized cry I had heard, but I would need to hear her again to better pinpoint her location. I listened carefully as I went around the car to the driver's side, but I heard nothing unusual. Perhaps she'd been taken indoors, where the wind couldn't pick up her voice. Beyond knocking on every door in Findale, I had no other way to find her.

Jason was right about it being too early to go home, and I didn't especially want to be alone. I drove to the shop instead, hoping that Cormac would still be downstairs. The showroom was dark except for the security lights, but I could see a sliver of light shining from under the workroom door. I turned my key in the lock and let myself into the store.

Two things hit me as I entered: the sound of merriment among friends and the savory aroma of something delicious. I had just decided to turn around and leave, not wanting to ruin anyone else's night, when the laughter died down. An unfamiliar voice spoke into the silence.

"A pilgrim from The Otherworld has arrived. She needs solace."

A tall, regal Sidhe woman with metallic lavender hair and deep purple faceted eyes rushed out of the workroom, Cormac and Michan trailing after her. Her flowy dress fluttered behind her as she approached me, giving her an angelic appearance. She gathered me into her arms and held me close to her like the mother I'd never had. The inner wall I'd built to hold my emotions in check dissolved in an instant, flooding me with fear and sadness. I sobbed against her cheek like I'd never allowed myself to do before while she hugged me, her cheeks damp with her own tears.

She pulled away as my sobs died out, holding me at arm's length. "Better?" she asked.

"Yes. I'm sorry, I don't know what came over me," I said, a bit embarrassed by my outburst. I wiped my cheeks dry with the palms of my hands.

"Aisling came over you," Cormac said with a chuckle. "This dear woman is an Empath."

"Come, we will warm your stomach with a good meal and you can tell us what has upset you so," Michan said, steering me toward the workshop.

I sat on a stool and let the three of them fuss over me. Michan ladled out a bowl of aromatic lamb stew packed with potatoes and vegetables. Aisling buttered a warm biscuit and placed it on a plate next to my stew. Cormac poured me a glass of red wine. Once they were sure I had everything I needed, they settled around the table and returned to their half-eaten dinners.

Only fifteen minutes earlier I would have said I couldn't eat a thing without upsetting my stomach. Michan's stew not only tasted fabulous, but it also felt comforting.

"Michan, I assume you made the meal? It's delicious. Thank you," I said, taking a bite of the light, fluffy biscuit. All eyes were focused on me. I knew what they were waiting for."Something tragic happened to someone in town tonight. I heard the most pitiful, anguished cry on the wind. Did any of you hear it?"

"We were here inside, so no, we didn't hear it," Cormac said. "Do you have any idea who it was?"

"A woman, that's all I can say. Aisling, her emotion was so intense. Surely you must have felt it?" I asked, a shiver running through me as I remembered the tortured sound.

"If I know someone well I might be able to get a general sense of their well-being from a distance, but I need to be in close proximity to read a stranger. I wish I could help this poor woman, but if I use my essence to ease the emotions of a human, I open their eyes to the fae. My brethren wouldn't thank me for rendering their glamour useless."

"Cormac, you've only been here a week and you already found me and two other fae. I've been here for months and have never run into any until now. How does that work?" I asked, hoping a change of subject would lighten the mood.

"Did you think you were alone?" Cormac asked.

"Well... yes. At least here in the Pocono area."

"There are always fae nearby," Cormac said with a chuckle. "You just need to know where to look for them. I put the word out that I needed a percussionist—"

"—and I answered his call," Aisling said, taking a sip of her wine.

"Okay, I'll bite. Why did you need a drummer?"

"Have you ever heard a modern ensemble without one?" Michan joined in the conversation, his excitement evident in his voice. It took an extra beat for me to understand the Brounie's meaning.

"Oh cool, you guys are forming a band," I said. "Michan on guitar, Cormac on whatever other instruments and Aisling on the drums. That's great." I marveled at the speed with which Cormac had put this together, just like so many things he had accomplished since he'd arrived.

"And you on the flute, but of course you'll need to continue taking lessons. You aren't particularly good yet."

"Cormac!" I said, annoyed that he'd made such a comment in front of others. Besides, it wasn't true; I considered myself a talented instrumentalist. A seed of panic grew in my stomach when it hit me what he was suggesting. "I didn't agree to this."

"You'll love it, my dear," Aisling chipped in. She reached out, covering my hand with hers, clearly sensing the change in my emotional energy. "The Sidhe are performers by nature. As soon as you're on stage you'll be fine; nothing compares to performing to a live audience."

My mouth dropped open; I couldn't imagine anything worse. It wasn't stage fright that worried me; I'd come back to the Human World to escape the notoriety I'd gained in Faery and to live in relative obscurity here. Living under that type of negative scrutiny would ruin the reputation I had established for myself in this town: an unremarkable person who most of the town never thought about unless they needed something fixed.

All three of them were looking at me with bright, enthusiastic eyes. I rubbed my forehead as I tried to decide which would be worse: performing or disappointing my friends.

"We were just getting ready to practice. Try it out for tonight and see how you like it," Cormac suggested.

"I don't have my flute." Cormac reached around and pulled my flute case from the counter behind him.

"What about Max?" I squeaked, my desperation growing. "I need to get home to let him out."

"Asleep upstairs with Padraig."

No other arguments came to mind. I took a deep breath, exhaling in a huff as I admitted defeat—at least temporarily.

"Fine. I'll practice with you tonight, but I make no promises about being a part of this whole thing."

CHAPTER 15

e spent hours playing music that night, after which Cormac insisted I sleep on the couch in his apartment since I would have to come back in a few hours to take Padraig to school anyway. Despite the comfy sofa, fluffy pillow and soft blanket he provided for me, I had a restless night. Every time I closed my eyes, the heart wrenching wail played over and over in my mind. What could have happened to have caused such agony? When the sun finally peeked through the living room window, I was grateful to have an excuse to get up and start the day.

A fresh set of clothing lay in a pile at my feet. *Thanks, Michan*, I thought, picking them up and tiptoeing to the bathroom. Having a Brounie around meant always being well taken care of. I emerged from my quick washup feeling refreshed in a pair of clean jeans and t-shirt, but I needed coffee desperately.

Not wanting to wake the rest of the household, I slipped downstairs to the coffee station I had set up in my office. I tried to be patient as the coffee brewed. The instant it finished I mixed my perfect ratio of coffee to cream. I discovered a container of homemade chocolate chip cookies. *Michan strikes again.* I plopped into my desk chair and let the caffeine and sugar revive me.

I admired my upgraded workspace while I munched. The pride I felt in its new appearance took me by surprise; I hadn't even realized I cared about how it looked.

The cabinets we'd assembled created the outer perimeter of my space, which stopped short of the back wall near the entrance to the storage room, allowing enough space for a pseudo doorway. A child's gate attached between the back wall and the end cabinet gave me the option to close Max in and keep curious store patrons out.

Cormac had placed a smooth slab of granite on top, giving the cabinets a classy finish and creating countertop space for me to work. He had also swapped out my rickety old metal desk with a sturdy wooden one that was stained the same dark walnut color as the floors. We painted the boards on the front of the checkout counter a darker shade of yellow to contrast with the pale-yellow walls. Then Cormac inscribed the front with 'Murray's Appliance Repair' in stylish lettering. He built shelves on the back where I could store my tools within easy reach, but out of the customers' sight.

Padraig came running down the stairs and burst into the showroom with Max beside him. He wore the belted tunic and soft leather shoes typical of the fashion in Faery. Max dashed over to me and sprang into my lap for his morning hugs.

"I'm going to school today! I'm going to meet other kids!" Padraig yelled, his voice squeaking with excitement. "Did I tell you I'm in second grade?"

"Yes, I remember. I'm driving you over there," I said, brushing his hair out of his eyes and feeling charmed by his enthusiasm. "And you've only told me a hundred times, you're in second grade."

"Yay, I get to go for a ride in the car, too!" It hadn't occurred to me that he had yet to ride in one of the vehicles he found so fascinating.

"Where's your Uncle Cormac?" I asked.

"He's not upstairs, so he must be working," he said, standing on his tippy toes to reach in the bin for a cookie. He trailed behind me as I headed towards his uncle's workroom.

"Two questions," I said, poking my head in. "Did you even go to bed last night? And did you get the kid any human clothes, like I asked?"

"Good morning, Sloan," Cormac said, looking up from the wooden pieces of the violin he was varnishing.

"Yeah, I'm sorry," I said, taking a deep breath and exhaling slowly. "Good morning, Cormac. I'm afraid I didn't sleep very well last night." Cormac nodded, mollified.

"I bought the clothes, but he refused to wear them," he said, looking pointedly at Padraig. The little boy shrank under his stern gaze.

"I don't like those tight pants," he whined. "They're uncomfortable."

I shook my head; the kid had no idea the teasing he was in for. Second graders were old enough to pick on each other's differences. "Fine, but I'm guessing you'll change your mind tomorrow.

"Paddy, would you take Max out to the side yard for his morning walk? I need to speak with your uncle for a minute."

Boy and dog raced out the door together as Cormac set down his brush and looked at me with curiosity.

"There's someone else I need to check out as a possible suspect, if you don't mind," I said without preamble. "He's an employee at the pharmacy who has more or less disappeared. The timing is suspicious."

"What do you know about him?"

I thought back and realized I had precious little information on the man. "His name is Douglas Simmons. He's in his late twenties to early thirties, and um… That's about it."

Cormac's eyebrows shot up his forehead. "That's not a lot to go on. Do you know if he lives in Findale?"

"Is he good looking?" Aisling's voice preceded her into the room. She came through the door with a flirty grin on her face. "I'm acquainted with every good-looking guy in town. If I haven't met him, I'll know someone who has."

"Aisling, what are you doing up so early?" Cormac asked.

"I'm not up early, I'm going to bed late." She turned her attention back to me. "Who are you looking for?"

"Douglas Simmons," I said. She shook her head.

"I don't recognize the name, but I can find him. Why are you looking for him? Did he leave you in the lurch, Sweetie? You don't seem terribly upset about it if he did."

"No, nothing like that," I said as I tried to will the blood away from my blushing cheeks. "I'm sure you heard about the pharmacist's murder?"

"Well yes, but I never believed for one minute that you killed him."

I sighed. Somewhere deep inside, I had hoped she hadn't heard about it—that I still remained anonymous to the late-night crowd.

"Well, we're trying to figure out who really killed him before the police come and haul me away," I said.

"Oh no, we would never let that happen!"

"Over my dead body!" Cormac and Aisling spoke at the same time. I put up my hand to stem their outburst.

"I know, I know, and I appreciate you guys having my back, but I'd rather clear my name. If it does come down to going on the run, I'll be a fugitive here in the Human World. I'd have to go back to Faery, too, and that's just too big a sacrifice."

Aisling came and hugged me. "What can I do to help?"

"Don't you think it's suspicious that no one remembers seeing this guy after the murder? Could you find out where he is and what he's up to? I want to know why no one at the pharmacy has been able to get ahold of him."

"I can do that," she said, stretching her arms and yawning. "But first, I need to get some sleep."

We watched Aisling leave, her gait so graceful she seemed to float, a few seconds later the bells over the door jingled. Cormac glanced at a clock on the wall and grimaced.

"There's something I have to tell you," he said. I frowned. *Now what?* His demeanor suggested I would not like whatever was coming next. "We've been engaged to play at JR's, the eating establishment on Main Street."

"Yeah, I'm familiar with the place. What do you mean, 'we'?"

"Our ensemble. We'll be playing every Wednesday and once a month on Fridays."

I shook my head as if I needed to clear out my ears. I couldn't have heard him right. "Did you have this information last night?" I asked, glaring at him.

"Well... I didn't get confirmation until this morning." At least he had the decency to look guilty. "The person responsible for getting us the gig should be here any minute, so I wanted to be sure you knew about it now," he said.

"I didn't agree to this," I said, gritting my teeth and staring him down.

"We're having a practice session this afternoon after you bring Padraig home from school," Cormac continued as if I hadn't said anything. He closed his varnish and cleaned his brush, ignoring the stink eye I was giving him. "You don't want to spoil this for everyone, do you?"

"Cormac, that's not fair," I shot back as the doorbells jingled again. Still grumbling, I went to greet the newcomer.

In the showroom, Padraig was sitting at my desk eating another cookie. Max sat next to him, his big brown eyes begging the boy for a taste. For a moment I thought the two of them had rung the bells on the front door, but then I spotted Tommy in his police uniform. He was facing away from me, admiring a display of concertinas.

"Do you play?" I asked, rearranging my face into my customer service smile.

"Oh hey, kid! Staying out of trouble?" he asked, just as he always did at the café. His eyes danced; he was trying to get a rise out of me. With my already frayed nerves, I couldn't stop myself from reacting.

"Seriously, Tommy? I am *NOT* a kid."

"Yeah," he said with a chuckle, "and I guess I shouldn't joke about trouble anymore… But it's not my fault you look like a twelve-year-old."

I sighed. I didn't look that young, but this time I wouldn't take the bait. Surely joking with me was a good sign, compared to ominous warnings to get a lawyer? It occurred to me that this was the perfect opportunity to feed him my ideas about other suspects in Walter's murder.

"Tommy, have you guys investigated any of the pharmacy's past employees?"

"You guys?"

"You know, the police. I heard Walter didn't treat his staff very well. Apparently he fired one of them, Ed Parker, when his girlfriend got pregnant. He's still bitter about it. There's also a Douglas Simmons, who seems to have disappeared. Nothing says guilt more than running, right?"

"Look, Sloan, I'm not a detective, so I'm not involved in the investigation… but I'm not the enemy either. Seriously, I'm on your side. I'll pass along the suggestion; I hope it helps."

"Good morning, Tommy," Cormac interrupted our conversation. "The good officer introduced us to the people at JRs," he told me in an aside. "You brought the contract?" he asked.

"You instigated this?" I asked, stunned.

"Well, the owner's son is a buddy of mine and they needed another group in their lineup. It seemed like a no-brainer to ask Cormac if he was interested. I thought you'd be happy — I understand you have a great voice."

"You misunderstood. I'm the flutist," I said. I glared at Cormac, doubly annoyed that I just unintentionally labeled myself as a member of the group.

"Aye, Tommy, you got it right. Flutist and lead singer," Cormac said.

"Wait, what? I've never done any singing. What makes you think I'd be okay with that — or that I'd be any good?" I inched toward the door. Any more surprises and I might explode. "Come on, Padraig, we need to get going."

Cormac laughed. "Of course you have a lovely voice, and I guarantee you'll love performing. After all, you're a Si —" he glanced at Tommy — "born to it."

"We'll talk about this later; I have to get Padraig to school," I said, heading for the door. Before we could get outside, a phone rang. Max barked as if outraged by the disruption.

"Sorry, I have to take this," Tommy said, stepping away from the rest of us. As he listened to whoever was on the other side of the call, his expression went from apologetic to serious to alarmed. "I've got to go. Police business." He was still on the call as he ran out the door.

CHAPTER 16

"*P*adraig, put your seatbelt on," I said for the second time as the little boy excitedly messed with the fan settings on the dashboard. "You don't want to be late on your first day, do you?"

He sat back and pulled the seatbelt across his stomach. "Now what do I do with it?" he asked. I reached over and grabbed the end, showing him what to do by buckling it for him.

"You push here to take it off," I said, pointing at the release button.

He held on to the door armrest with one hand and clutched his seatbelt with the other as I started driving, only to let go a few blocks later. He crossed his arms and pouted.

"It doesn't go nearly as fast as a dragon," he said, his voice laden with disappointment.

"What?" The word dragon jolted me free of my deep thoughts.

"The car doesn't go as fast as a dragon."

"Have you ever ridden a dragon?"

"No, but I've seen how fast they go."

"Well, you're right. The car is slower, but it can move faster than this. One of these days I'll take you for a drive on the highway," I told him. "Let's go over the things you must remember not to talk about with people in school, like dragons. What else?" I asked, questioning the wisdom of letting this little guy loose unsupervised in an entire building of humans.

He sighed, obviously tired of going over this. "Leprechauns, Sidhe or any of the other fae, Faery, The Otherworld," he recited.

"Talk about all the great things here in the Human World," I advised, but then a thought struck me. "Just be careful not to mention that you haven't actually seen those things before."

He laid his head against the car door, looking forlorn.

"Listen, it's okay if you slip up once or twice. We can chalk that stuff up to an active imagination. There's only one thing that you must absolutely always make sure of."

"Keep my glamour up," he said mechanically.

"Exactly," I said, navigating around the yellow school buses and pulling over in front of the school. I turned to give him my full attention. "I know you're tired of hearing it, but look at me and tell me you understand how important this is."

"Hey, there's Miss Gregory! She's my teacher," he said, pointing to an older woman with salt and pepper hair who stood at the entrance to the school. He had talked about her constantly since meeting her when Cormac enrolled him in the school.

"Padraig," I said, demanding an answer before I would let him go.

"I understand. Can I go now?"

"Not until you give me a hug," I answered with a smile. He stood on the seat and gave me a quick embrace before opening the door and hopping out.

Max jumped up from the backseat and tried to follow Padraig out of the car. I grabbed his collar and held him in place while Padraig pulled his backpack up from the floor. Stuffed with the supplies the school had told us he needed, the bag looked heavy enough to tip the small boy over.

He slammed the door shut and waved before running up to a group of children in front of the building. They appeared to accept him well enough. I waited until he was safely inside before pulling away from the curb and heading toward the Apple Dumpling to check on Emma. Max, his escape route gone, curled up and fell asleep on the seat next to me.

I sat at a red light, waiting for the opportunity to turn onto Main Street. While I watched for a break in the passing cars, my mind wandered back to Cormac's crazy plan to have me be a member of his band. Maybe I could convince him that I could be the manager, or a roadie— something behind the scenes that the public would never notice.

I was so wrapped up in my thoughts that I almost didn't see it.

A red pickup truck drove past in the midst of the other traffic. My heart pumped with excitement as I craned my neck, trying to see if the passenger-side bumper had any telltale scratches, but I couldn't get a good view. Adrenaline surged through me; I couldn't lose him if there was even the smallest chance it was the same truck. I gunned the gas and hurried to make the turn, cutting off a silver sedan who blasted his horn in anger. Max sat up at the sound and barked, pressing his nose against the side window as he looked for the source of the noise.

I swerved across lanes to get closer to the truck, the sudden shift in direction knocking Max back down onto the seat. I had nearly caught up to it when the pickup turned right off Main Street. As it turned, I spotted the familiar damage to the bumper: proof that it was the same truck that had dropped the backpack. I took the same right and flew after it, following it through the next intersection just as the traffic light turned from yellow to red.

The pickup sped up, aware now that I was tailing him.

I tried to look for clues to identify the driver, his face in the mirror, the color of his hair—anything. But it was hard to see through the tinted back window. It looked like it was a man, judging by his height and the breadth of his shoulders, but the color and length of his hair was hidden beneath a baseball cap.

A siren wailed as blue and red lights flashed in my rearview mirror. A police cruiser sped along behind me. *Good*, I thought. *He can take this guy to Detective Moody.*

The road twisted, curving first left and then right. I took the curves at a reckless speed, determined to keep up with the truck. Max whined as he struggled to stay put. The police car fell behind, lights still flashing.

The further we got from town, the denser the vegetation grew until it began to overtake the shoulder of the road. We had started into another curve when the pickup made a sharp right turn onto a gravel road hidden from sight by the dense foliage. I tried to make the turn, but I was a split second too late and going a little too fast. The Mustang spun out on the gravel, the back wheel sliding into a ditch with a clang.

I flung myself out of the car, leaving the door wide open as I ran to stare after the truck. *Shit! I should have gotten the license plate number*, I thought belatedly, squinting through the billowing cloud of dust. It was no use; I couldn't make out a single digit. After a few seconds, the truck disappeared from sight.

The police car cruised to a stop on the opposite side of the dirt road from where my Mustang had landed. Max, miraculously still in the car, started barking incessantly. Officer Clark got out and approached me slowly, holding his hand out as if to calm me.

"Sloan, I need you to get back in the car."

"Did you see it? Did you see the truck? It was the same one that the backpack fell off. He could be Walter's killer, you need to go after him!"

"What I need is for you to get back into your car."

It finally hit me how nervous I was making him. I probably sounded crazy. He held his right hand over his pistol, ready to draw it if necessary. I took a step backwards and stumbled over something hard on the ground. The spearhead, I was sure, had materialized for my protection. but I refused to look down at it and risk bringing it to his attention. If he saw that I had a weapon, the situation would only get worse. I didn't even want to think about what would happen if he realized that it the same blade that had disappeared from evidence.

I took another step back, dragging my foot and knocking the blade into the ditch.

"I'm sorry, Officer Clark, I didn't mean to alarm you. I'm getting back into my car."

Luckily, Max was able to diffuse the tension. He recognized the officer when he came around to my window and asked for my driver's license. Max put on the charm, his wagging tail making his whole butt wiggle as he climbed over me to reach the officer. He panted up at him, his tongue hanging out the side of his mouth.

"I see you're still learning how to be cooperative," Officer Clark said to me as he patted Max's head. "When a policeman flashes his lights, you pull over-- pronto."

"Yes, sir. I've learned my lesson." *Ha! There's cooperation for you,* I added silently.

CHAPTER 17

I drove back to town, grumbling under my breath. *So stupid...* It wasn't the twenty-minute lecture or the two tickets Officer Clark had given me that I was upset about; I knew I'd gotten off easy for my reckless behavior. It was the fact that I'd lost sight of the pickup truck without learning any information that would help me track down its driver. Why hadn't I thought about getting the license plate number?

I parked in the alley behind the café, planning to pop my head in just long enough to ask Emma what had happened to her last night and make sure she wasn't upset with me. I'd filled up on cookies and coffee earlier, so I didn't need breakfast.

I entered to find a silent, empty kitchen, something that had never happened before. The usually spotless kitchen was in disarray. Baking sheets filled the sink to overflowing, waiting for someone to load them into the dishwasher. A fine layer of flour covered the center of the worktable, which had been left unwashed after rolling out the last batch of pastry. An unbaked pie lay abandoned on the counter next to the hot oven.

A murmur of voices came from the dining room, but I couldn't tell whose. I tiptoed toward the doorway, worried about what I would find on the other side.

Two of Ida's employees were perched on the stools on the customer side of the counter, hugging each other and weeping. A few locals sat at the tables along the window, expressions subdued and voices low. As usual, the local gossips sat at the round table in the middle of the dining room. Today, however, Ida was sitting with them, dabbing a napkin to her eye.

The only person standing was Tommy, still in his navy police uniform and holding his hat in his hands.

"Tommy, this can't be true!" Ida wailed. "Emma was a good girl, a happy girl with a bright future. She wasn't depressed. She wouldn't have killed herself."

My breath froze in my chest.

"Ida, I'm so sorry to bring you this horrible news," Tommy said. "I never meant to imply that Emma was anything but a nice young lady. We believe it was an accidental overdose, not a suicide."

I gasped, loud enough to draw everyone's attention. Could Emma have been that upset about Jason that she killed herself? The idea sounded insane, but if what Ida said was true...

"Emma's dead?" I asked in a whisper, hoping I had heard wrong.

Tommy frowned and gave me a grim nod. My breathing became short and rapid, on the verge of hyperventilating.

"Oh Sloan, sweetheart. You two were close, weren't

you?" Ida said, taking my hand and guiding me to a chair. She sat down next to me and held my hands in hers. "Okay, now you need to slow down your breathing. Take a deep breath and let it out slowly."

She inhaled and exhaled along with me until my breathing regulated. I felt the eyes of everyone in the café boring into me as I worked to control my emotions.

"Now, tell me the truth. Are you using drugs too?" Ida asked. "If you are, we can get you help before something awful happens to you."

"What?" I asked, my sluggish mind struggled to understand. I was still trying to process the fact that my friend had died, perhaps while Jason and I were waiting for her at the bar.

"We've already lost three young ladies to drugs this month. I don't want to lose another one. Are you using any drugs?" she asked again.

"No, and neither was Emma. Not street drugs, anyway. She was only taking the prescription meds the doctor gave her for her wrist injury."

"What about you, are you taking any prescription drugs?" Tommy asked, his gaze zeroing in on me. A tear dripped from my cheek onto my t-shirt, leaving a dark wet spot.

"No! I don't understand what's going on. Can someone please tell me what happened?" It didn't make sense. Emma hadn't looked good yesterday, but she had gotten her medicine. The drugs should have made her feel better.

"She overdosed on her pain medication," Tommy said.

"Her poor dear mother found her on the back patio

last night," Ida interjected. "The poor thing thought Emma had fallen asleep until she couldn't shake her awake."

"She screamed so loud we heard it over at our house —we live next door, you know," Gladys said. "My George ran over and had to call the ambulance. Her mother was shaking uncontrollably and couldn't do it herself."

I closed my eyes, my tears leaving streaks down the sides of my face. I thought I might throw up as I remembered the tortured wail that had come to me on the wind.

"The EMTs took Emma to the hospital," Ida resumed, her voice cracking as her own grief swept over her, "but they couldn't save her, poor thing. This place won't be the same without her."

A hush fell over the café as everyone ruminated over how Emma's absence would affect them. Ida suddenly stood, indignant.

"What's happening to our town? So much tragedy in the past few weeks—first the Newburg sisters, then Walter and now Emma." Tommy grimaced as if he knew what was coming next. "The police better find this killer before all the tourists get chased away. Nobody wants to visit a drug infested, murdering town."

"We're doing our best," said Tommy. "Once again, I'm sorry for your loss." He turned to leave.

Ida's mention of Walter's murder reminded me that I had more information to pass along to Tommy. Although Ida reached out to stop me, I rushed to follow him as he went outside.

"Tommy, wait!" I called. He leaned against his cruiser, scowling as he crossed his arms over his chest.

"Sometimes I wonder why I'm so nice to that woman," he said.

"Because she gives you free shoofly pie and was good friends with your grandmother?" One side of his mouth crooked up.

"Oh yeah, that's it." His expression turned somber again. "Are you going to be okay?"

"Unfortunately, this isn't the first time I've lost a friend. I'll find a way through it. Right now I need to speak to you about something else."

"What's up?"

"I saw the red pickup truck again this morning. You know, the one that the backpack fell out of. I followed it to try to get a look at the driver."

"You did what?" he asked with a scowl.

"Don't worry, Officer Clark stopped me before I could do anything too stupid. I didn't get a good look, but I can say for sure that it was a guy, not Tasha. Unless they're accomplices, in which case—"

"Listen, Sloan. You have got to leave this investigation to the professionals."

"Not while I'm the primary suspect," I snapped. Tommy rubbed the back of his neck, looking tired although his shift had just begun.

"I shouldn't tell you this, but Moody told me you're not the *lead* suspect anymore."

"I'm not?"

"No."

"But I'm not cleared yet?"

"Well, not totally… but they're starting to look at other people."

"Like Tasha?" I asked and he nodded. "Did you tell

them about the ex-employees? Ed Parker and Doug Simmons?"

"I've been dealing with Emma's death since we last spoke, but I promise you I'll let them know." He walked around his cruiser.

"And about the pickup driver being a guy? Maybe one of the ex-employees owns the red pickup."

He nodded again as he got in his car. I tapped on the window closest to me and he pushed the button to lower it.

"Didn't the Newburg sisters die of an overdose too?"

"Yes."

"Did they have the same doctor as Emma?"

"Think so, but I'm telling you: don't get involved. You'll only get yourself into more trouble. The police are already looking into it."

*T*he brisk breeze made the air chilly, but I couldn't stand the thought of going back into the café and facing the scrutiny of everyone inside. Instead, I walked around the block to the alley where I had parked the Mustang.

Jason was waiting for me there, leaning against the wall. He hadn't worn a jacket and so he stood with his shoulders hunched and his arms crossed in front of him as he tried to stave off the cold. I hesitated for a second, not sure how I felt about finding him there, before continuing toward him.

He straightened when he saw me approaching, his red-rimmed eyes imploring me to hurry to him. I picked up my pace, feeling an urgency to share our mutual grief. He gathered me into a hug and we both wept again.

"This is all my fault," he said, his voice heavy with pain.

"What do you mean?" I asked, pulling back from his embrace enough so that I could see his face.

"The medication yesterday. I should have waited for the pharmacist to check it." He stared into space, eyes unfocused.

"Do you think you made a mistake? Could you have given her the wrong drug or the wrong dosage?" He shook his head. "So even if you had waited, the pharmacist would have given her the same thing. I don't see how that would have changed what happened. It wasn't your fault, Jason."

"Then why do I feel so guilty?"

"Because you're a nice guy, and she was your friend. Come on, let's go inside and get you a hot drink to warm you up." I put my arm around him, intending to escort him into the café. He held his ground, wiping the tears from his face with the palm of his hand.

"Thanks, but I have to get to work."

"Are you sure? Maybe you should call out today." He didn't look like he was in any shape to be waiting on customers, with his emotions written all over his face. "I'll drive you home if you'd like."

"No, I'll be okay. Besides, Tasha is depending on me." He squared his shoulders, pulling himself together mentally and physically.

"Okay, if you're sure. At least let me drop you off? It's too cold to walk."

CHAPTER 18

*M*ax kept Jason preoccupied by demanding his attention as we drove the few blocks over to the pharmacy, leaving me to brood over what had happened to Emma. My grief took on an edge of anger. I needed to find out who had prescribed those drugs to her and why so many people were dying from the very thing that should have helped them. Someone had to put a stop to it.

My adoptive father taught me that if you need to learn something new, you go to the library. I had spent countless hours of my youth researching in our local public library, but I hadn't visited one in years.

"Where's the closest library, do you know?" I asked as we pulled up to the pharmacy. Jason's brow creased as he contemplated the question.

"I've seen one over on Chestnut Street. I'm not sure which block exactly, but it's somewhere south of Main Street."

"Thanks, that helps. Are you sure you don't want to go home?"

"Yes. I'm better off keeping busy." He reached for the door handle, hesitating for a moment. "When will I see you again?" he asked.

I bit my lip to stop myself from saying 'never,' not if he meant going out on a date. A relationship was impossible now; Emma's memory would always stand between us. "We'll see. I can't make any plans just now."

He nodded in silent acceptance, passing Max over to me and climbing out of the car. With a quick wave, I left him standing on the sidewalk watching me drive away.

I dropped Max off with Cormac and headed across town. I slowed as I passed Burt's garage, curious if I could see Jason's car. I spotted the red Mitsubishi parked off to the side, in desperate need of a wash if nothing else. A tinge of guilt passed through me; I could easily get the car running for him. But I had made a promise to Burt. I shook my head, pushing those thoughts away as I turned onto Chestnut Street two blocks later.

I drove up and down twice before spotting the sign for the library. No wonder I hadn't noticed it previously; I had been looking for a commercial building, but the library was located in a large, renovated, Victorian-style house.

The inside had the cozy feeling of a home, each room packed with comfy upholstered furniture and wooden shelving units piled high with books.

As a teenager eager to speed through my schoolwork, I had learned that the quickest way to get an answer for anything was to ask the research librarian for help. A young man re-shelving books directed me upstairs when I asked where I could find her.

The walls of the original rooms on the second floor had been removed to create an open area to house the reference section, giving it a stark, bright feel. Wooden tables and chairs had been arranged throughout, creating the perfect environment for studying. The librarian sat at a U-shaped desk at the top of the stairs. Her large brown eyes looked up from her computer as I approached.

"I need to learn about why or how people die from prescription drug overdose," I said, struggling to find a concise way to describe the information I needed. She nodded and stood.

"You're asking about the opioid crisis? The local paper's been running a good series on it since the recent deaths." She walked me over to the area displaying newspapers and magazines and pointed out today's paper. "I'll grab the back issues for you."

She returned with a stack of papers, the top issue bearing the headline 'National Opioid Epidemic comes to Findale.' I thanked her and sat down at a table to read them. The first story was from the day after the Newberry sisters died.

Most of the top half of the front page was taken up by a sweet picture of the girls, both in their twenties, with their long dark hair pulled away from their faces, dressed up for a special occasion in pretty dresses and wearing radiant smiles. The article began by detailing the incident that had led to the girls' use of opioids. They had been in a car accident that spring, careening off the road during a downpour. The older sister, the driver, had a broken collarbone from the shoulder strap of her seatbelt. The younger girl broke her leg, a result of the car crashing into a tree on the passenger side. They had both suffered from depression while dealing with their injuries, but friends and family claimed that they had long since recovered.

I skipped the parts about the family's reaction to their deaths. Parents losing both their daughters, a boy losing both his sisters all in one terrible night— it could only be a recap of pain and regret. I didn't need to add any more grief to my own right now.

The police had ruled their deaths to be suicide based on several clues, but the main reason seemed to be their disbelief that both girls could accidentally overdose at the same time.

The article mentioned the name of the doctor who had prescribed the opioids, Orthopedic surgeon Dr. Larry Greenwood. He claimed to have stopped prescribing the pain killers to the sisters at least two months earlier. Greenwood insisted they must have either stockpiled the drugs or bought them off the street.

Didn't Parker say something about a Larry? Something about filling his prescriptions? I wondered how it all fit together.

The newspaper series ran over the course of five days. I learned about the exponential growth of the crisis through the early 90s and the wide range of the problem, crossing all demographics, and the concern surrounding doctors over-prescribing the meds.

After reading three issues, I paused for a minute to process the implications. Emma had been addicted to painkillers and no one had known. Not me, not Ida, and evidently not her family either. The idea seemed unfathomable, yet it had to be true. I frowned and resumed reading.

A sentence jumped out at me from the fourth issue, turning my stomach: 'The risk of opioid overdose increases when returning to the drug after an interruption in use.' I closed my eyes and forced myself to take deep breaths to calm my overload of emotions—frustration, grief, guilt—and to stop my impulse to crumble the library's newspaper.

I hesitated to pick up the latest issue, knowing that Emma's death would be the focus of the article. As with the issue on the Newberry sisters, the front page displayed a picture of her at her best. She wore a pretty smile, her thick strawberry blonde waves cascading over her shoulder.

The article described Emma's fall and the subsequent surgery on her fractured wrist before retelling the dramatic story of the failed attempt to revive her. The name of Emma's doctor wasn't mentioned. *It must have been the same guy, right?*

I returned the newspapers to the librarian and thanked her for her help. I left the library determined to learn the name of Emma's doctor.

I waited at the curb in the same spot where I had dropped Padraig off that morning. Yellow school buses lined the surrounding street. A bell rang and the empty sidewalks were instantly flooded with a mass of children running to their buses or their parents, teachers yelling 'walk' to no avail.

I scanned the throngs of children, searching for mine.

I finally spotted him lagging behind the others, barely putting one foot in front of the other. His new backpack dragged on the ground behind him. I jumped out of the car and ran to meet him halfway, alarmed by his demeanor. I took Padraig's hand and hooked one of the backpack's straps on my elbow, rescuing it from the beating it was getting. We walked the dozen or so steps to the Mustang in silence.

"So, what's up?" I asked once we were settled inside, trying to keep my tone light.

"Nuttin," he mumbled, clicking his seatbelt into place.

I raised an eyebrow. First of all, that clearly wasn't true. Secondly, was he picking up slang already? Perhaps he would feel more inclined to talk once we were moving. I put the car in gear and pulled out of the parking lot.

"Padraig, I get the feeling something's bothering you. Do you want to tell me about it?" I asked. He faced away from me, staring silently out the window. I was about to rephrase the question when he spoke.

"The teacher told the other kids that I was special."

"Oh? Isn't being special a good thing?" I asked, not following.

"That's what I thought at first, but what she meant was that I'm different. I kept my glamour up, I promise I did, but I'm still not the same as them. I'm shorter than everyone else, and they said I talk funny and dress weird." I bit my lip; I had known the clothes would be a problem. We should have made him change. "All the other kids are the same."

"You know, Paddy, it may seem that way, but it's not true. There are many ways that you're the same as they are, and many ways that they are different from each other. You just need to look a little closer. Some of them probably have big noses or funny names. Besides, who says different is bad? You're short, but you can move faster than any of them. You hear better, too. One day your special talent will come out, like your Uncle Cormac's gift with crafting instruments."

"But I can't tell them about any of those things," he pouted, glancing at me from the corner of his eye. His expression had brightened a little, but I hadn't totally convinced him.

"That's right, you have a secret none of them get to know about. How cool is that?"

"That *is* cool." A grin spread across his face as the thought set in, and his normal bubbly personality returned. "Guess what we have in our classroom?"

"I can't imagine," I said as we pulled up in front of the store.

"It's an animal called a guinea pig! He's soft and furry and his name is Squiggles."

Padraig was inside the shop before I realized he'd left the car. He'd left his door wide open. I closed it behind him and locked up, following him inside with a bit of trepidation. Cormac had mentioned something about the band practicing after I brought Padraig home.

Cormac was waiting on customers inside: a teenage boy and his mother. The teenager was cradling one of the Leprechaun's exquisitely crafted guitars as he chose from the handful of leather cases to house it in. His mother, meanwhile, was discussing a lesson schedule and fees with Cormac. He paused his conversation to greet

Padraig as his nephew ran past him to go upstairs, then returned his attention to his customer.

I moved discreetly toward my makeshift office, trying not to disturb them, only to have Max come barreling out of the workroom, whining excitedly as he leapt into my lap. I was scratching behind his ears to calm him when I noticed a note laying on top of the desk, written in Cormac's elegant handwriting.

Tasha Lewis requests that you visit the pharmacy tonight at six to repair the register.

The shop door opened and Aisling sashayed in. She looked spectacular in denim leggings that showed off her figure and a lightweight, flowy pink sweater. Michan followed behind her, his guitar case in hand. The teenager forgot all about the cases when his eyes fell on Aisling. He ran his fingers through his blond hair, pushing it off his face and stretching his spine to stand an inch taller.

I smirked as I watched his reaction. Sidhe women often had that kind of effect on men—fae or human, although I seemed to be an exception from my experience so far.

"Do you play?" the young man asked Michan as he glanced sidelong at Aisling.

"I sure do, and you'll never find a higher quality guitar than Mr. Cormac's here. You're buying one for yourself?"

"Well, my mom's getting it for me."

"Why don't you play something for him, Michan?" Cormac asked. "Give them a taste of how the instrument sounds."

With mother and son engrossed with the other two

fae, Cormac made his way around the cabinet wall to join me in my office.

"You have been summoned," he said, pointing at his note.

"It's a good thing! Maybe I'll learn something that will help solve—" I cut myself off mid-sentence as Aisling began singing along with Michan's guitar. She had a full, luxurious voice that defied anyone not to pay attention. "Why not make her your lead singer?" I asked.

"Wait. You'll see."

I closed my eyes to focus solely on her lovely voice. It took a few seconds before I started catching on to the lyrics. She sang from the perspective of a dying young woman who was asking her loved ones not to mourn her short life, but to celebrate the time they had with her. *How did she know?* I wondered, snapping my eyes open again. I blinked rapidly, trying to hold back the tears I felt welling up in my eyes.

Aisling met my watery gaze and dipped her head, acknowledging my grief. Her voice cracked, tears flowing freely down the side of her face until she couldn't continue singing. The teenager's mother wrapped an arm around the Sidhe to comfort her.

"Now imagine her performing in a bar," Cormac said. "A song like that is bound to raise emotions in more than one person. It's too much for her; she becomes a basket case. It's less intense somehow when she isn't the one singing, but you'll have to get used to her overreacting to some extent no matter what you sing. That's why we keep her in the back with the drums."

"I don't know, Cormac. I'm still not convinced I'm the right person…"

CHAPTER 19

A closed sign hung in the pharmacy window when I arrived at six o'clock sharp. The store was empty; neither Tasha nor Jason in sight. I tried the knob and was surprised to find that it turned freely. Not the smartest idea, leaving your door unlocked while alone at the location of an unsolved murder. Then again, maybe she knew she had nothing to worry about…

"Hello?" I called as I stepped inside.

"I'm in the back," Tasha called, her voice drifting out from the business office.

I put my tool chest on the counter next to the register and joined her. She sat leaning back in the leather desk chair, her stocking feet propped up on one of the office chairs, a glass of red wine in her hand. Her heels lay abandoned on the floor beneath her legs. She had cleared a spot in the middle of the cluttered desk to make room for a takeaway container of lasagna and a bottle of wine.

"I ordered dinner from the Italian place down the street. There's plenty, would you like some?"

"No, thanks."

"Suit yourself," she said, taking a sip of wine. "Can I offer you a glass? Or maybe a soda?"

"I'll pass on the wine, but a cola sounds good." I grabbed a bottle from the refrigerator in the store and settling into a second, miraculously clutter-free chair. Perhaps I could get her talking if I sat with her for a while.

"You don't look any closer to getting through these papers," I said, glancing around.

"Oh, I've gone through them. Several times, as a matter of fact. The problem is that nothing makes sense. As horrible as Walter was, he was always a good businessman. He was exceptionally good with money."

It sounded odd to hear her refer to her father by name instead of as Dad. If her story was true, though, I couldn't blame her.

"I'm a numbers person myself; I have a degree in accounting. I've managed the finances at a large law practice for ten years now, and I can tell you with certainty: the figures here don't add up. The purchase orders are the most organized," she said, gesturing toward a two-drawer filing cabinet with a ledger on top. "The store's drug purchases this year are already significantly higher than they've been for the last two years."

"If he kept ordering more medications, business at the pharmacy must have been going well, right?" I nodded to show I was following her story.

"There aren't any records from the cash register, presumably because it hasn't been working. Just hundreds of these handwritten receipts." She glared at the pile of cardboard storage boxes on the far side of the office, each overflowing with illegible slips of paper.

"Someone was putting sales numbers into these ledgers, but it wasn't Walter—it's not his handwriting. Jason told me Walter had trouble writing after his stroke, so Doug filled the books in for him. If these numbers are correct, massive amounts of drugs are missing. I did an inventory myself just to be sure. If he sold them but neglected to record the sales, what happened to the money? It didn't go into the pharmacy's bank account."

"Perhaps he hid it somewhere?" I suggested as she took a bite of her dinner. "You know, he could have stashed it under a mattress or buried in the yard. He had a lot of cash in that backpack; maybe he was planning to take it to his hiding place."

She laughed, not out of amusement but contempt. "Maybe. He sure knew how to keep things hidden."

She picked up a large yellow envelope, faded with age and thick with paper, and tossed it over to me. Although dying of curiosity, I hesitated to open it until she gestured her consent.

It took me a minute to work out that the documents were copies of notes from a police investigation. A teenager named Donna had fallen down the cement stairway to the family's basement. Her mother, Barbara, accused her father of pushing the girl.

"Is Barbara your mother?" I asked, trying to put the pieces together.

"No. Nor is Donna my sister. Well, I guess she's my half-sister but I'd never heard of her before. Looks like

Walter had a completely different family before he met my mom. I'm sure she never knew about it; she would have told me if she did."

"What happened to the girl?"

"She cracked her head on the cement floor at the bottom. Amazing that she didn't die, but she had severe brain damage and ended up in a wheelchair. Guess that's what it took for wife number one to leave the abusive bastard. The divorce papers are in there too; it all took place the same year he moved here from Syracuse and met my mother."

She drained her glass and refilled it from the bottle on her desk.

"Do you think Walter would really go that far? He would have to have known that a fall like that could kill her."

"The police couldn't prove anything, but I'm sure he did it. According to the mother, she had broken one of his stupid rules and the staircase was handy. It wouldn't have taken much to set him off: watching TV for a minute too long, not sitting straight enough in church. She broke a doozy this time: he found out that she had a boyfriend and they'd been sneaking off to the movies behind his back."

She lifted her glass with a sardonic smile. "To dear old dad, the absolute worst of the lot."

"I have plenty of experience with dysfunctional families myself," I said, feeling connected to her story. "I like to think of myself as the white sheep."

Tasha wrinkled her nose at the remaining lasagna on her plate and pushed it aside. "Enough of that; you came here for the cash register. The new one arrived after I left that message for you earlier, so you can take it tonight if you want," she said, standing and walking me over to it.

"This register was in the store when I was a kid," she said, nostalgia in her voice. She ran her hand across the top of it. "I used to like spending time here; it felt safe. There were still lots of rules here, but my father never lashed out in public. He called this store his legacy. How pathetic is that? Look at it now, nothing but a rundown, penniless sham. Now that I have my own kids, I understand what a fool he was. Your children are your true legacy."

She gave me a sad little smile. "I'm sorry, I didn't mean to ramble on like that. I'm sure you want to get out of here. Can I help in any way?"

"No thanks, I got it." Whoever had installed the register originally had bolted it to the counter. I took a screwdriver out of my toolbox and began loosening the screws that held it in place.

"I'll get the door for you." Tasha picked up my toolbox and rushed past me as I picked up the heavy machine. As soon as I passed her, she let the door go, rushing ahead of me again to open the door to the Mustang.

I set the register down on the passenger seat.

"Are you sure you don't want something for it? I didn't fix it in time for you to use it." She waved me off.

"It's not necessary. I'm glad just to get rid of it," she said, waiting on the sidewalk as I rounded the front of the car to the driver's side door.

"She had a child," she blurted suddenly, as if the need to reveal this detail wouldn't be denied. "Years later."

"Sorry?" I asked, not following. "Who?"

"Donna. Somewhere out there, I have a nephew."

CHAPTER 20

ormac and Michan had tackled painting the wooden trim of the store's exterior, making the outside of the building look as fresh and clean as the inside. They had artfully arranged instruments in the front window, creating an enticing display. The street-light reflected off the metal of the guitar's tuning pegs and the tacks around the top edge of a bodhrán. For the final touch, they added gold lettering to the windowpane that read 'Murray and Fitzgerald' in large letters. Under-neath in smaller letters were the words 'Murray's Appli-ance Repair' and 'Fitzgerald's' Music'.

I had to grin. Leprechauns don't use surnames; they choose one for themselves only when dealing with humans, who expect everyone to have one. Cormac's choice of Fitzgerald could only be a nod to me; the name meant son of the spear carrier. He was decades my senior, but the sentiment spoke of love and family.

The store was closed and dark, only the overhead

security light illuminating the showroom, but it was light enough for me to see finishing touches they'd added inside during the short time I'd been away. To the left there was a new glass display case filled with replacement parts: strings, reeds, mouth pieces, drumsticks and the like. A specially designed rack along the back wall held rows of sheet music anthologies and books on music theory. The music store felt complete and in order, an incredible upgrade from its appearance when Cormac first arrived. He must have really milked his deal with Michan for them to have gotten all this done so quickly!

I carried the cash register inside, depositing it on the counter in front of my office area. I stretched my back, relieved to be free of the heavy machine. The soft glow of light filtering in from the workroom further illuminated the darkness. Assuming I would find Cormac there, I went to join him.

Cormac was facing away from me, concentrating on making long, even strokes across a plane of wood with a piece of sandpaper. A steaming mug of tea sat on the worktable, out of his way but still within reach. Padraig was asleep in the far corner of the room, curled up on a large pillow on the floor with Max asleep beside him. I paused for a moment, taking in the scene of Leprechaun-style domestic bliss.

"Are you okay?" Cormac asked in a low voice without looking up from his work. I sighed in response, settling into a soft upholstered chair in the corner close to him.

"It's been a long day."

"I'm sorry about your friend. Were the two of you very close?"

"It's hard to get close to someone when you have to hide so much about yourself from them, but I considered her a good friend." I pulled my feet up on the chair and wrapped my arms around my knees.

"Aren't you afraid to let him nap for too long?" I asked, looking over at Padraig. "He'll be up all night if you do."

"Nothing could have prevented it. His day at the human school exhausted him—so many new sights and sounds." Cormac stopped working to peer over the table at his nephew. "His experience didn't dissuade him. He wants to continue going. I'm not sure what my sister would say." He grimaced and shook his head.

"She would be happy that Padraig is happy. They'll teach him reading and writing, and in his off hours you can instruct him in the ways of the Leprechauns." Cormac nodded and returned to his sanding.

"Aisling stopped by on her way out for the evening. She wanted to tell you that she has located someone who knows the man you're looking for, and that she'll meet up with him tonight."

"Oh, okay, that's good," I said. I had nearly forgotten that she'd said she would ask around about the missing clerk. It felt like it had been days since we'd had that conversation, rather than that very morning.

"And how went your visit to the pharmacy?" Cormac asked. He wiped the piece he was working on with a soft cloth, holding it up to the light to check for imperfections.

"We have a new cash register for the shop, I just need to overhaul it a bit. It's a lovely machine," I said, taking an extra moment to gather my thoughts. "Walter Strum was not a good man, but I don't think it follows that Tasha killed her father. She distanced herself from him and didn't even come back when he needed a caregiver. Once you know the whole story, who can blame her? I can't see any reason she would come back now to get revenge."

"I agree," Cormac said. "To all appearances, she has a good life in New Jersey. Why risk losing everything?"

"But something hinky is going on—or *was* going on— at that pharmacy. Tasha told me that a large quantity of drugs is unaccounted for."

"Perhaps finding their way into the hands of a few vulnerable young ladies? I can see that," said Cormac, nodding.

"That guy who used to work for Walter—the one I saw at the bar. He mentioned someone named Larry. It sounded like he was implying that Walter had some kind of problem with his prescriptions. I bet you all three girls who died probably had the same doctor: an orthopedist named Larry Greenwood. If Walter had threatened to expose him—well, the doctor might have killed him to keep him quiet."

Cormac stopped working to give my idea some thought. "It's an interesting theory, but don't you think the authorities would have investigated him if all the girls overdosed on medications prescribed by the same doctor?"

"Probably, but would they connect all of that with Walter's murder?" I sat up straight, placing my feet back on the floor. "What if I make an appointment with him? We'll make up some kind of story. I'll go in complaining of pain and see what he does."

"What would that prove?"

"I don't know. Maybe nothing, but it's worth a try."

CHAPTER 21

I arrived at the three-story office building that housed Larry Greenwood's medical practice early the next morning. I made a pass around the parking lot on the off chance that I would find the red pickup. Once satisfied that it wasn't there, I parked and went in search of his office suite a few minutes ahead of my appointment time.

There were four names listed on the glass door to the practice, including Greenwood's. Patients crowded the waiting room wearing expressions ranging from boredom to concern, watching the television hanging on the wall or playing with their phones.

An elderly gentleman who had arrived before me walked up to a glass window and spoke to the woman on the other side. Following his lead, I got in line behind him. The doctors' credentials were displayed near the receptionist's desk; Greenwood's medical degree from Upstate Medical University certainly looked legitimate.

"Name, please," the receptionist said when my turn arrived.

"Sloan Murray; I have a 9:30 appointment."

"Fill out these forms and bring them back to the window when you're done," she said, handing me a clipboard and pen. "Do you have your insurance card with you?"

"I don't have insurance," I said, biting my lip. Going to the doctor was a new experience for me; my father had occasionally taken me as a child, but I had never been to a human physician as an adult. Would she turn me away for not having medical insurance?

"Okay, just fill out the forms and bring them back. You'll have to pay for the visit when you're done." She pointed to a sign taped to the glass stating that payment was due at the time of service.

Relieved, I filled out the paperwork using the story Cormac and I had created the previous night after making the appointment. I had just relocated to Findale from out of state. I was recovering from foot surgery and my pain meds were running out. The form asked how long it had been since I'd had the surgery; I chose six months—not too long ago, but long enough for me to be off medications. I was curious to see if he would refuse to give them to me, or if he'd maybe refer me to a rehab and try to help me get over the addiction. I didn't expect that he would.

A few minutes after I returned my completed paperwork to the receptionist, a middle-aged woman wearing blue scrubs came into the waiting room and called out my name. I followed her down the hallway to exam room five.

"So, what brings you here today?" she asked as I settled into the exam chair.

I repeated the information I had just written on the form, which made me wonder why they had insisted I fill it out in the first place. The nurse stared at a computer screen, taking notes as I spoke.

"Okay, thank you. I'm going to take your vital signs before Dr Greenwood comes in."

Sheer panic ran through me as she wrapped a blood pressure cuff around my arm; Cormac and I hadn't thought this part through. I had no idea how close a Sidhe's vital signs were to a human's, nor did I know if my glamour would coverup any differences.

The nurse didn't react unusually in any way that I could see. Her expression remained neutral as she finished taking my blood pressure. She took my temperature and pulse next, typing the numbers into the computer without comment.

"Just relax here for a minute, okay? The doctor will be with you shortly," she said, putting the blood pressure cuff back in its holder and leaving me alone in the exam room.

I took advantage of the alone time to look around. A poster on one wall diagramed how metal pins were used to repair a broken femur. Another advertised a brand of soft casts. The only attempt at adding artwork to the room was a print with nothing but blocks of color in various sizes.

The room felt cold and impersonal. In The Otherworld, the sick were treated outside as often as possible to connect them with the healing forces of nature. Healers would give a part of their fae essence to restore their patients, and the innate power of the natural environment completed the job. Their essence is what gives the Sidhe their sparkle: their pearlized skin and bright, faceted eyes.

The room was furnished with a double cupboard and a small sink installed in the countertop. There was a flyer next to the sink listing the local pharmacies in the area, with Strum Pharmacy circled in red. A light tap on the door startled me; I stuffed the list into my jeans pocket and sat down in the chair again as the doctor entered.

I recognized him immediately: Dr Greenwood was none other than the blond man in the lab coat who had been outside the pharmacy on the day of the murder. He wore a similar coat now. Up close I could see that he was younger than my first impression; he couldn't be much past thirty, if not in his late twenties. He sat on a leather-topped stool and rolled towards me, stopping a respectful distance away.

"Hi, I'm Dr. Greenwood," he said, reaching out to shake my hand. "I see you had surgery a few months ago. Your doctor still has you on pain medication? Were there complications?"

"No, I guess it's just taking it a long time to heal. It still hurts like crazy."

He stood and put the ends of his stethoscope into his ears. "I'm going to take a listen, okay?"

I nodded, leaning forward so he could place the head of the stethoscope on my back. From this new angle I noticed an NFL poster on the front of a lower cabinet: The Buffalo Bills.

"Are you from upstate New York, Doctor?" I asked.

"Yeah, what gave me away?"

"I saw your degree on the wall in the reception area and now the football poster there," I answered, gazing at the poster and thinking hard. A new theory was forming in my head.

"Very observant. I'm from Westvale, New York; born and bred. Go Bills," he said with a smile. His eyes were surprisingly warm and friendly, making me feel guilty for coming to his office under false pretenses and even guiltier for suspecting him of murder.

He sat back down on the stool. "Let's take a look at your foot. Which one is it, the right?"

I wasn't sure if I should expect a thorough examination from a doctor who was quite possibly running a drug scam, but I had planned for this possibility. My right foot had a two-inch scar on the bottom from an old injury. I was reaching down to take off my shoe when a commotion erupted in the hallway.

"What the heck?" Greenwood spun on his stool. "Sloan, give me a minute please," he said, rushing out the door to investigate.

I followed him, curious to know what was happening outside. A dozen law enforcement officers crowded the hallway, Will Clark among them. A female agent stood in front of Dr. Greenwood, the letters FBI emblazoned across the chest of her uniform.

"You can't go in there," Greenwood snapped at the two officers going into an office on the left side of the hall.

"This says we can," said the FBI agent, holding up an official-looking document. "This is a search warrant for this medical practice. There's another being executed at your home as we speak."

"I'm calling my lawyer."

"Good idea, but you'll have to wait. Lawrence Greenwood, you're under arrest for Medicare fraud, false or unnecessary issuance of prescription drugs and corruption related to kickbacks."

I slipped past as they handcuffed him, intent on getting out of the building before I got caught up in this new mess. I made it as far as the door to the waiting room unnoticed, only to find Detective Moody blocking my escape. He shook his head as I approached.

"Like a bad penny, you just keep turning up. What are you doing here? You're involved in this drug scam too?" He was baiting me and I knew it, but I couldn't keep myself from biting.

"Don't be ridiculous," I snapped. "I was here for an appointment just like all the other patients. I'm as innocent as they are." His eyes narrowed in response to the insult; perhaps calling him ridiculous hadn't been the best move.

He took a step closer and jabbed me with his index finger. "Who are you? Is Sloan Murray even your real name?" I pressed my lips together as he spoke, praying that the spear wouldn't decide I was in trouble and appear at my feet. "I did some digging and there's no record of you anywhere, other than your driver's license and a few notes on an old shoplifting case. No birth certificate, no school records, not even a prior residence. Where did you come from?"

"There's no big mystery," I said, laughing in an attempt to hide my fear. My false amusement enraged him, his face turning a bright and angry red. "I was a foundling, adopted and homeschooled in New Jersey.

It's not my fault if there aren't any legal records. It wasn't my responsibility to report my own adoption to the government."

"There's something fishy about you. Mark my words, I *will* figure it out," he threatened, turning away from me in disgust.

I rushed out of the building, shaking from my encounter with the detective. It took several deep gulps of the fresh air, helped along by the natural energy radiating from the plants outside, to ease my pounding heart. Would he ever leave me alone, even if they solved Walter's murder? I shouldn't have antagonized him.

I scanned my surroundings for Cormac; we had agreed last night that he would post himself somewhere close in case our plans went south. I spotted him at the far corner of the parking lot, peering over at me with concern written all over his face. He raised his eyebrows to ask if I needed help. I shook my head and jutted my chin towards my car, telling him with two simple gestures that I was fine and I was leaving. He nodded and left, moving so quickly he seemed to disappear.

Jason jogged up, startling me as I walked past the multiple police cars clustered around the entrance to the building.

"Sloan, my god! Are you okay?" he asked, giving me a quick hug. "What's going on in there?"

"They're arresting the doctors, or at least Dr. Greenwood. I don't know about the others," I said without slowing my pace. I wanted to put as much distance between the detective and myself as possible. It took me a moment to realize that Jason wasn't beside me anymore. He had turned to stare at the scene unfolding behind us, joining a small crowd of patients and passersby doing the same. Police officers carried out boxes and piled them into a van. The FBI agent escorted Dr. Greenwood out in handcuffs, placing him in the back seat of a squad car.

"What are you doing here, anyway?" I asked from where I had stopped. "Shouldn't you be at the pharmacy?"

"I was waiting on my Uber when I saw all the police cars. My apartment's not far from here." He caught up to me and walked me to my car. "I had to come down and see what was going on, but I guess I'm gonna be late now."

"Hop in, I'll give you a ride."

There were two more police cars at the pharmacy when we pulled into the parking lot. Jason jumped out of the car, slamming the door behind him in his haste to get inside. He blew right past Tasha, who stood wringing her hands just outside the door.

"They say Walter was running a drug scam with one of the local doctors," she explained when I joined her. "He might have been responsible for the death of that young woman the other day. Yet another life destroyed by that man."

"Do you think he did it?" I asked. She shrugged.

"He always acted like he was holier than thou, but I wouldn't put it past him. Behind closed doors, he was evil."

We stepped inside together and saw Jason standing in the pharmacy area. He was being questioned by a man in a dark suit—a police detective, FBI maybe. Both men wore grim expressions.

"What do you do here? What are your duties?"

"I'm a pharmacy technician. I can fill prescriptions under the supervision of a pharmacist, which is what I spend most of my time doing," Jason explained. "I wait on customers, too. Ring them up and that kind of thing."

"What about submitting insurance claims and dealing with the money stuff?" Dark Suit asked, leaning in toward Jason just a fraction of an inch.

"No, not me," said Jason, waving the idea off. "I don't know anything about insurance claims; Doug and Walter handled all of that."

"Doug?"

"Douglas Simmons. He was the office manager, and he also took care of customers after I left for the day. Tasha's been doing it recently."

"Sloan?" Tasha's voice interrupted my eavesdropping. She stared at me quizzically; I must have missed something she said.

"I'm sorry, I was distracted. Does the name Larry Greenwood mean anything to you?" I asked, debating with myself whether or not I should share my latest theory with her.

"No. Why? Should it?"

"He's one of the local doctors. The police arrested him while I was at his office this morning." I glanced around; no one was close enough to hear me. "I found this in the exam room." I dug the crumpled flyer from my pocket and handed it to her. "He's been encouraging his patients to come here. It might be a stretch, but I'm wondering if he might be your nephew, Walter's grandson. He's the right age, and he comes from upstate New York."

"So you're saying my nephew might be as awful a person as my father? Great," she sighed. "I can't wait to get away from all of this and go back to my family."

Jason came out from the back, his face pale and drawn. Tommy followed behind him, carrying a box of files. He met my eyes but didn't otherwise acknowledge me as he continued out the door.

"They say Walter was running a drug scam," Jason said. "I can't believe it!"

"Well we can't open the store now, Tasha said. "You should go home, Jason." He furrowed his brow as if this hadn't occurred to him.

"Are you sure? I can help you clean up once they leave…"

"No. I'm done with this place; it's not worth all this trouble. I'll pay you for the day and I'll give you a good reference, but I'm closing the pharmacy down for good."

Jason opened his mouth to argue, but Tasha's expression was resolute.

"I guess I'll head over to the Apple Dumpling and see what the gossips are saying about all this," he said, shrugging. He headed out the door, crossing paths with Tommy as he came back inside.

"Mrs. Lewis, we're all done here," said Tommy. "I'm sorry to put you through all this. I know you've been through a lot lately."

"Thank you, Officer. Do you think all this is linked to his murder somehow?" Tommy glanced at me before answering.

"We'll be looking at every angle until we figure out who killed him."

"You know what I don't understand?" she asked. "If my father was running a scam, where's the money? As far as I can tell, he was flat broke."

"People find ways to hide money when they want to," Tommy said. Tasha and I shared a glance; he had echoed my suggestion from the night before. Another officer diverted Tasha's attention and I took advantage of the moment to pull Tommy to the side.

"Tommy, did Tasha tell you that Walter had a family before he met her mother?"

"No, why?"

"She told me she just found out that she has a nephew. I think Larry Greenwood might be him."

"She told you he was?" he said, glancing over at her.

I shook my head. "I'm just making an educated guess; she doesn't actually know his name. Maybe Walter was going to report him, or maybe Larry wanted revenge for all the abuse Walter put his mother through." Tommy shook his head.

"Sounds a bit far-fetched to me, but I'll see what I can find out about Greenwood's parents."

CHAPTER 22

*M*ax ran to greet me as I entered the store. He jumped up and planted his front paws on my knee, wagging his tail as frantically as though he hadn't seen me for a month. I picked him up for a quick hug before setting him back on the floor.

"Sloan, a hotel called to ask about their carpet cleaners," Cormac called out from the workroom, making no comment about the morning's drama.

I cursed under my breath. One of the local hotels had sent over three commercial vacuums in need of repairs. I had promised to have them ready by that afternoon, but I'd completely forgotten them with everything that had been going on.

I grabbed the first one, the easiest to repair. All it needed was new belts. I made quick work of it and moved on to the second one which needed a motor rebuild. As I was taking it apart, Cormac pulled up a chair to the far side of the cupboards and began playing his guitar.

"What are you doing? Entertaining me while I work?"

"No, I'm accompanying you." He said, strumming a few chords. "You don't seem to realize it, but you sing while you work—all the time. That's how I know you'd make a great lead for our ensemble." He plucked a note and frowned, and tuned the string quickly as he spoke. "Just let me give you a few lessons to improve your technique, that's all you need. We're practicing again tonight, then we're heading over to JR's for a mini session. Our first real performance is on Friday. You want to be ready, don't you?"

"You expect me to sing in front of people? *Tonight*?" I squeaked, my voice an octave higher than usual. He shrugged off my concerns.

"It's a Tuesday night; the place will be empty. You just need to tweak a few fine details, anyway. I'll have you ready in no time."

Panic constricted my throat. I didn't want to disappoint him, but I treasured my relative obscurity and I didn't want that to change.

"No time for a lesson today. I have to finish fixing this vacuum, and I have another one to fix when I'm done," I said, scrambling to find an excuse.

"No worries; I can teach you while you work."

"Fine," I sighed. He would not let it go.

We sang old folk songs together, songs we used to sing around a campfire with our troupe of Leprechauns back in The Otherworld. It was a bright memory from what had been a very dark time. Cormac followed up with instructions between each song.

"You can sing longer phrases if you take low breaths. You know where your diaphragm is, right?"

"Yeah, it's a muscle below my lungs."

"Correct. It's connected to the muscles around your middle too. Put your hands on your sides and imagine breathing into that space. You should be able to feel those muscles expanding, along with the diaphragm. You'll be able to take in more air that way, but remember to control how you use it."

I did as he instructed, and the difference proved remarkable. I could take deeper breaths and hold the phrases for longer. The sound felt stronger somehow too.

"Wow, that's a neat trick. Thanks."

An hour and several songs later, the third vacuum was finished and running smoothly.

"You have a natural talent you don't find in the Human World, Sloan. If you decide to take this seriously, you could be a sensation," Cormac said as he laid his guitar back in its case.

"No thank you. The last thing I want is to be famous," I replied. "That's the exact reason I don't want to sing in public. That was fun, though," I added hastily, seeing how deflated he looked at my response. "We could do that again anytime."

I placed my tools back on the shelves and set the vacuums out of the way. "I need to call the hotel and let them know the vacuums are done, but after that I'm going to work on the cash register. Do you want to keep going?"

"Later. I have a student coming in soon to take a fiddle lesson."

Taking his words as a precaution, I closed the gate to

my shop to trap Max inside before his student arrived. I used the telephone on my desk to call the hotel to inform them they could pick up the vacuums any time before six pm. Cormac's student, a nine-year-old boy, dragged himself into the store with little enthusiasm. The two of them disappeared into the classroom.

Alone and finished with my paying work for the day, I shifted my attention to the register. The outside was in excellent condition. I assumed that it wouldn't take much to get the inside working again, seeing as the exterior had been so well maintained. A simple mechanical over-haul should do the trick—clean and lubricate, and perhaps replace the motor drive gears. I unscrewed the casing with great anticipation. After removing the screws I prepared to wrestle with it to take off the cover, assuming that years of grime and dirt would have cemented the edges to the cabinet's insides. Much to my surprise, it came off so easily that I stumbled backward, fighting to keep my balance.

As I placed the outside cabinet on the counter, sour notes from Cormac's novice student drifted out from the classroom despite the closed door. Max whined to voice his dislike.

"Don't you dare start howling, or you'll have Cormac to contend with," I scolded.

I turned on the radio sitting on my desk to drown out the disagreeable noise before leaning down to inspect the register's insides. I wasn't sure the clash of the two sounds was much better, but I left the radio on anyway and went back to work.

"What's this?" I mumbled, noticing that someone had jammed several wads of a mysterious gray substance into the gears. I tentatively touched one of them with the tip of my finger, then snapped it back. Gum. Someone had gunked up the mechanism with chewing gum. This couldn't be an accident; someone had put this register out of commission on purpose.

"Why would someone sabotage the cash register?" I asked out loud to no one.

Max jumped onto my office chair, tail wagging, under the misapprehension that I had spoken to him. I scratched behind his ears while I mulled over my discovery. If this had anything to do with the drug scam, it seemed unlikely that Walter was a co-conspirator. More likely, someone had done this to hide something from him—like how much of the money that was coming into the pharmacy never made it into the cash register.

The shrill of the phone ringing jarred me away from my thoughts.

CHAPTER 23

I dropped the receiver on to its cradle and sprinted into the classroom, barging in without bothering to knock. Cormac and his pupil looked up in surprise at the abrupt interruption.

"There's trouble at the school," I blurted, running back to my desk to grab my forgotten keys.

Cormac hurried the boy out to his mother, who had been waiting in her car while her son had his lesson. He apologized profusely, promising to reschedule as I hustled Max out of the shop and locked up.

"I knew no good would come from having that boy mix with Humans," Cormac said, shaking his head in disgust.

"Maybe it won't be that bad," I said, lifting Max off the driver's seat and setting him in the back as Cormac and I climbed into the Mustang.

We sped down Main Street and onto Market, only slowing when the flashing lights of the emergency vehicles came into view. A firetruck and a police cruiser were parked haphazardly along the side of the school near the playground. The emergency vehicles had drawn yet another crowd.

"Geez, what a spectacle," I grumbled, resigning myself to the fact that I would be in the police's sights once again.

Cormac jumped out before I could put the car in park. I cracked the windows and followed close behind him, leaving Max inside. I caught up with the Leprechaun just as he stepped onto the sidewalk across the street. Miss Gregory, the gray-haired teacher Padraig had pointed out to me on his first day, rushed over to meet us. We kept moving, forcing her to scurry along behind us.

"I'm so sorry. I don't know how he got up so high. There was a teacher on recess duty, but she didn't see him until it was too late."

The windows along the rear of the school were plastered with the faces of teachers and students watching as we pushed through the crowd around the fire truck. Tommy stood with his head dropped back, gazing up at a tall tree on the edge of the playground.

"It's okay, buddy, we're coming to get you. I need you to hang tight for now though, okay? Don't try to come down on your own."

Padraig was sitting on a branch a good twenty feet up the tree, partially obscured by branches covered with yellowing leaves. Even from this distance, I could tell that he was shaking all over. I groaned. A human child could conceivably have climbed to that height, except for the fact that there weren't any limbs for the first five or six feet of the tree trunk.

"Yes, sir," the small Leprechaun answered, his voice thin.

I saw the moment he spied his uncle. An odd combination of relief and apprehension crossed his face. He knew he was in trouble, but he also knew he could trust Cormac to get him out of this mess.

"He has to stay there until they rescue him, otherwise there will be too many questions," I whispered to Cormac. I watched Padraig, hoping he could hear me as well. He nodded, eyes wide with fear.

"I don't think he could safely get down on his own anyway. He's never attempted falling from anything close to this height before," Cormac whispered back. This gave me a new, more terrifying worry: a fall from that height could kill the boy if he didn't land right. My heart leaped into my throat.

A uniformed firefighter maneuvered the large red firetruck, steering it as close as possible to the tree. He cautiously extended the ladder on the back toward Padraig.

"Tommy," I called out as I moved closer to him. "Will they be able to reach him with that thing?"

"They think so, but they might have to remove a few branches from the tree to get close enough to grab him. We need to make sure he stays put until they reach him.

"You stay here and keep him calm. I'll be back." Tommy hustled over to the firetruck without waiting for a reply. Cormac, disregarding his instructions, followed close on his heels, leaving me alone to keep an eye on the boy.

Padraig stared at the rig rising toward him. He started to shimmy around the tree trunk, trying to get to the side closest to the ladder. Suddenly the ladder's top rung hit a thick branch, the tree swaying from the impact. One of Padraig's feet slid off the branch. The crowd collectively gasped in fear.

"Stay still and hold on tight," I called up to him, forcing my voice to stay calm despite the nerves jumping around in my stomach. "They'll be there soon to help you."

He gingerly sat on a sturdy branch, clinging to a smaller one just above it.

Cormac approached three firefighters who were huddled together watching as the ladder inched closer to Padraig, stopping a foot away from him.

"Gentlemen, I'm sorry we have put you through this inconvenience. Please allow me to climb the ladder and retrieve my nephew. He will be less anxious and less likely to cause more trouble if I'm the one who comes for him."

"I'm sorry, sir, I can't allow that. The Chief would have my hide if I let a civilian on the truck."

"I'll go up," Tommy said. "The boy knows me." The firefighter opened his mouth to argue, shrugging as he changed his mind and stepped aside to let Tommy get past him.

Padraig seemed to be getting tired; it looked as though he was shifting his weight to try to ease his sore bottom. Someone had to get to him before he wiggled himself off that branch. Tommy trotted up the ladder, not hesitating for a second as he climbed up over two stories high.

"Okay Padraig, I want you to hold onto that tree until I tell you otherwise. Can you do that for me?"

Padraig nodded, keeping his focus on the policeman. Tommy gripped a handle on the top of the ladder with one hand before leaning forward and wrapping his free arm around Padraig's waist.

"Okay, let go!"

Padraig obeyed and Tommy scooped the boy away from the tree, holding him snugly against his chest as he steadied them both. He shifted Padraig in order to hold him more comfortably and began to make his way down the ladder. The crowd whooped and hollered, cheering him on as he made his descent.

Padraig ran to his uncle the second Tommy set the boy's feet on the ground. Cormac crouched down and caught him in his arms, squeezing him tight and whispering in his ear. Padraig frowned and nodded, taking his uncle's hand and pulling him along as he scooted back to Tommy and the firefighters.

"Thank you for saving me," he said in a tiny voice. "I'm really sorry for getting stuck up there. Is there any way I can make it up to you?"

The man in charge smiled at him. "You don't need to make it up to us. It's our job to help people."

"You gave him a great gift. There must be a way he can repay it," Cormac said.

"Okay, let me think. Why don't you come by the Fire Station after school tomorrow and we'll find a few chores for you? Will that do?" He looked over Padraig's head for his uncle's approval.

"That will be fine."

The crowd dispersed as the firefighters packed up their truck and drove away. Tommy departed with the last of the spectators, telling us he would see us later.

Miss Gregory tried to apologize again, but Cormac placed the blame where it belonged: with his nephew. He led Padraig over to me.

"Please take him to the car and wait for me there," he said. "I need to speak with the school officials."

"Sure, no problem."

Max greeted us enthusiastically, oblivious to the gravity of the situation that had just transpired. Padraig settled into the back seat and stared out the window, not even smiling when Max licked his cheek.

"Do you want to tell me what happened?" I asked.

"I didn't mean to jump that high, I promise. And I didn't drop my glamour, not for one second." He sounded close to tears.

"I believe you, honey."

"We were at recess and the other kids were playing a game to see who could jump the furthest. I only meant to jump a little way, but then the wind caught me. I couldn't help it!" He began crying in earnest. Max whined, nudging him with his paw.

"Don't cry, Padraig. Everything will be alright."

Cormac opened the passenger side door. He must have moved at Leprechaun speed; I hadn't seen him come out of the school or cross the street. I watched him out of the corner of my eye as I pulled away from the school, not knowing how he would react to the boy's breach. He said nothing for several long, agonizing minutes. He finally spoke as we pulled up to the store.

"I would say the experiment has failed. I will home school you from now on."

CHAPTER 24

*A*disgruntled pre-teen girl with curly blond hair and glasses was leaning up against the building near the front door when we pulled up to the store, flute case in hand.

"I'm sorry I'm late, Hannah," Cormac said as he unlocked the door. "We had a slight emergency. Thank you for waiting," he said, gesturing her inside before him.

I followed behind, holding the door open for Padraig and Max. Once inside, we scattered in different directions. I headed towards my office while Cormac and his student went to the classroom. Padraig took Max back to the workroom, no doubt to plop down on his oversized pillow.

To my surprise, Aisling was sitting in my office chair, munching on chocolate chip cookies. Aisling was a notorious night owl; it was unusual to see her out and about at this time of day.

"You're eating my cookies."

"Michan made them, so I think that makes them fair game," she replied, taking another bite.

"How do you know Michan made them? Maybe I bought them at the Apple Dumpling," I said, suppressing a grin.

"Only a Brounie could make a simple cookie this delicious."

"Wow, I won't tell Ida you said that!" We both chuckled. A moment later, Aisling's expression sobered.

"I have news for you," she said. "Doug Simmons didn't kill the pharmacist, but he's probably responsible for the stolen money." I leaned back against the granite counter behind me and crossed my arms, astounded by her conviction. How could she be so sure?

"How do you know all this?"

"They arrested him in New Jersey the night before the murder for running the same scam at a pharmacy in Dover. He's been singing like a canary ever since."

"Singing like a canary?"

"That's what they say in all the gangster movies," she said with a grin.

"Okay, this is good news. It narrows down the suspect pool, right?" I sighed, trying not to think about how convenient it would have been if she had uncovered evidence that Doug was the killer.

"Sorry, Duck." Aisling stood and patted my cheek, instantly easing a touch of my disappointment. She grabbed two more cookies. "I'm going upstairs to see if Cormac has any milk. See you later."

I watched her flounce off through the door before turning my attention to refurbishing the cash register.

The flutist, one of Cormac's more accomplished

students, played the soft airy notes of *Two Dances* by Beethoven. The music was an excellent backdrop to my work, making it feel almost effortless. I cleaned the components of the machine that were salvageable and jotted down the parts I needed to replace: the pieces clogged with chewing gum, several other levers and all the sealing rubber.

While I worked, my mind went over and over what I'd learned about the dealings going on over at Strum's Pharmacy and who might have killed Walter. Despite Aisling's news, my gut told me that a connection existed between the murder and the drug scam. If only we could find it…

I thought back to the conversation I'd overheard at the bar between Jason and Ed Parker. It sounded like Ed may have been working with the doctor, filling the prescriptions for him, in which case I was certain he had been part of the scam. What had made Walter continue filling the scripts after firing Ed if he had been so against it in the first place? And where did the red pickup fit in?

The arrival of a hotel employee interrupted my thoughts. I helped her load the vacuums into the back of her SUV. Not long after she drove off, a couple came in to browse the instruments, whispering ooh's and ah's over the beautiful craftmanship. At some point Cormac's flute lesson ended, although I didn't notice the girl when she left.

Browsers and customers kept us busy until we closed shop at six o'clock. Cormac felt gratified with his two guitar sales, topped off with numerous smaller purchases. I had a sewing machine and VCR camera dropped off for repairs.

"The rest of our bandmates will arrive in about an hour. We should eat our dinner," Cormac said. "I'm sure Michan has left something upstairs for us."

"You have Michan cooking for you now?" I asked. "I thought I smelled something good."

"Ha! As if I could stop him."

"Aisling's already upstairs. I'll get Padraig."

I went to the door of the workroom to call Padraig for dinner. He sat on the pillow with Max asleep beside him. Scattered around them were colorful pieces of paper about the size of a postcard. Max opened his eyes and wagged his tail as I entered the room.

"What do you have there, Padraig?" I asked, moving closer.

"I found them in the back of your car. They were in here," he said, handing me a bright orange envelope exactly like the ones I had seen in Strum's backpack. The only difference was that this envelope showed no signs of the wear and tear the others had. I scooped a larger white envelope from the floor.

"Where did this come from?" I asked, staring at an address written at the top. It looked like the envelope had been used to process some sort of purchase; there were dates stamped on it, recent days from earlier this month. A big sticker in the middle of the envelope listed a price, tax and total.

"The orange thingy was inside the white one, and these were inside the orange one. What are they?" Padraig asked.

"They're photographs. Humans use something called a camera to capture a moment in time, and this is how the pictures look when they're printed out."

I'd never had much interest in looking at photographs. Human cameras were made to focus their lens so the images appear sharp to the human eye. My fae eyesight allowed me to see so much further than humans, but that meant their photographs always looked soft and fuzzy to me. I imagine it's much the same as a farsighted human looking at something close up. I picked up one and tried to decipher the image.

It was a woman in some type of open-air vehicle but the background didn't fit that scenario. The photo had been taken in someone's living room, rather than outdoors. There was something in front of her, but I couldn't quite tell what. Padraig handed me a couple more and I began to piece it together. The woman was sitting in a wheelchair with a small boy standing in front of her. In another shot he sat on her lap.

I moved the photo varying distances in front of my eyes, trying to bring the picture into focus. I stared at the boy's face, struggling to convince myself that what I thought I saw wasn't real. I didn't want to believe it.

"Padraig, your uncle wants you to come to dinner," I said, stuffing the photos back into the orange envelope and sliding it and the white one into my back pocket. "Tell him I'm going out to check on something. Worse comes to worse, I'll meet everyone at JR's."

CHAPTER 25

I drove along the same road I had taken the day I'd followed the red pickup. I drove past the dirt road where I had spun out the last time, continuing for another mile before making a right onto a paved road at the next intersection.

Dusk was falling and the back road didn't have any streetlights, but I kept my headlights off anyway, hoping to arrive at my destination undetected. I was confident that as a Sidhe with superior vision, I could see well enough to avoid any potential collisions. I travelled another mile without passing a single building of any kind. When I reached the address written on the white envelope, I pulled the Mustang onto the shoulder next to a line of hedges and parked there, hiding the car from view to anyone at the house.

The windows of the old farmhouse, which had been painted a cheerful sky blue, were dark. The side yard was full of tall trees, one with a swing hanging from a sturdy branch. A picnic table lay nestled among the trees nearby.

It was dark inside the detached garage, but one of the doors stood open. It appeared I had been lucky enough to arrive when no one was home.

The leaves on the surrounding trees rustled in the strong breeze, many of them blowing free and tumbling to the ground. The serenity of the place felt at odds with the unease that was coiled inside me. I crept over to the garage, glancing behind me several times along the way.

It was there. Inside the garage. The red pickup truck with the telltale scratch on its bumper. I edged up to the front passenger door, planning to check the glove compartment for the registration or insurance card to find out who its owner was.

I kicked something hard as I shuffled forward. Lugh's Spear spun away from the impact of my foot. I tensed, focusing my senses to locate the danger that must be close by, but sensed nothing off. The spear wouldn't appear for no reason; I decided it would be pragmatic to keep it with me. I was leaning over to grab it when something hit the back of my head. Hard.

I was sitting on the ground and leaning against a tree trunk when I regained consciousness, my hands tied behind me with rope. Jason stood by the picnic table, examining the photographs he had taken from my jeans pocket. He looked at them one at a time, placing each photo on the table in turn as if creating a huge collage. The spearhead lay on the table next to the photos. He had found it. If he tried to use the ancient weapon on me, I wouldn't survive.

"This is the first time I've seen these. I found an undeveloped roll of film, and naturally I was curious. I developed them through the service the pharmacy used." He continued flipping through the photographs.

"She was a wonderful woman, you know," he said, staring lovingly at his mother's image. "She never complained once about being in that chair."

I tried to loosen the knots that bound my wrists, but I only succeeded in tearing up my skin. I ignored the pain and kept trying.

"She sounds lovely," I said, figuring if I made nice, I might get out of there alive.

"As long as I can remember, my grandmother and my mom told me it was a car accident. Grams died maybe ten years ago, but it wasn't until my mother passed that I found the newspaper clippings and the information about the police investigation. They called it attempted murder."

"That must have been a terrible shock."

"How could anyone be so cruel, let alone to his own daughter?" He made eye contact with me for the first time.

I held his gaze, pushed my fae essence into my voice and said, "Jason Briggs, you will untie me this instant and let me get in my car and drive away."

"No," he said, furrowing his brow and staring at me like I was crazy.

Damn —Jason Briggs wasn't his real name. Without being able to true name him, I couldn't hold *Dominion* over him. I could no longer count on what had been my best shot of getting out of this mess quickly and easily.

"So, what? You came looking for revenge?" I asked.

"No. Well yes, I suppose I did. When Larry and Doug approached me about the insurance scam, I thought skimming off his business would be enough. It was easy money and lots of it, enough to buy this place," he said, nodding over to the house.

"How did it work?"

"Larry would send over prescriptions for patients he wasn't seeing anymore. I would fill them, and Doug would bill the insurance companies whether or not anyone ever picked up the drugs. The money from the insurance company only made it into the pharmacy's account about fifty percent of the time. If the customer didn't come for the drugs, Doug sold them on the street."

"So what? Walter figured out what you guys were up to?"

"The old man was glad to let us handle everything while he sat in his office and did nothing—never bothered to check my fills. Things were going so well; I didn't plan to kill him." He dropped the remaining photographs onto the table. "I had—borrowed—that backpack from him a while ago. Walter found it that day in the corner of the pharmacy and started snooping. He laughed when he saw her in the wheelchair. He *LAUGHED*!" Jason roared, his face contorted in fury.

I didn't know what to say to that; it had been an unspeakably cruel thing to do. My mind raced as I tried to come up with a different plan to get away from him. Another powerful gust of wind flew by. I pushed my voice into it and said, "I see you have my blade. You found Lugh's Spear." If by any chance one of my friends was outside and able to hear the wind, the sacred weapon's name would be sure to catch their attention.

"My one piece of bad luck, dropping that damn back-pack." He was lost in his own world now—not seeming to hear my remark about the spear. "I was thrilled at first when they accused you. They weren't even looking for anyone else."

"So you pursued me?" I asked, finding no logic in his behavior.

"When I met you at the cemetery, you took my breath away. You're so beautiful, Sloan. Then I realized you were searching for my truck to hand me over to the cops." He sneered at me, disdain written all over his face. This guy really was crazy. "I had to keep tabs on how close you were getting to the truth."

"So what now?" I asked, still pushing my words into the wind and hoping someone would hear me. "You already have Emma on your conscience in your effort to get revenge. Am I next? Are you going to use that spear-head on me?"

His eyes blazed. "Emma wasn't my fault! She begged me to give her those drugs." His lip curled. "I knew people would blame me for those deaths. I didn't force those girls to keep coming back for more. All I did was fill the prescriptions that were sent to me by a licensed physician, and that's not illegal." He picked up a pistol from somewhere out of my sight and pointed it at me. "Now you're making me get rid of you, when that's the last thing I wanted."

A large something fell from above Jason's head, landing on his shoulders and toppling him over. He flung an arm out as he tried to keep his balance, the gun went off with a deafening crack. Padraig, who had dropped from the tree, fought to keep Jason off balance. While Jason was struggling to get the little Leprechaun off him, Padraig managed to kick the spear head and send it skidding across the grass in my direction. I felt a tug on the ropes securing my hands. I peeked behind me and discovered Michan fumbling to undo the knots.

I leapt for the spear as soon as my bindings fell away, more afraid of its power in the wrong hands than I was of the gun. A swift movement to the left drew Jason's attention. His eyes grew wide when he spotted Cormac, whose bow and arrow pointed directly at his heart. Jason stopped trying to throw the boy off, clamping him in his arm and pointing the gun at him instead.

"Jason, think about what you're doing!" I cried. "He's just a boy!" The wail of sirens blew to us on the wind, growing louder as they came closer. "Don't let this whole horrible situation turn you into your grandfather."

He hesitated as he digested my words. His grip on the boy softened a fraction, giving Cormac the opportunity he needed. He used his Leprechaun speed to run unseen at Jason, whisking his nephew away to safety. Jason spun and pointed his gun in all directions, looking wildly for the boy.

If I threw the spear at him, I knew it would hit its target and kill him. That was how the magic of Lugh's Spear worked, but I didn't want to kill him. I would prefer to let the police handle the situation, as long as we could all get away unharmed. In the instant I formulated this thought, Aisling appeared behind Jason. She grabbed the wrist of his gun hand, draining him of all the emotion that fueled his behavior. She took away the hate, the fear, the anger and the grief until he crumbled to the ground into a puddle of tears.

Aisling stumbled backwards. She took a few deep, stuttering breaths before spitting out a string of curse words, her knees buckling under the weight of the emotions she'd just absorbed. She managed to regain her feet in time to stop herself from falling to the ground.

Jason looked up at the circle of fae surrounding him in horrified shock. "What kind of freaks are you people?" he spat out as two police cruisers sped into the driveway. Aisling's essence had broken our glamour, turning him into a Sidhe Seer: a human who sees the fae for what they are.

The other fae disappeared, leaving me alone with Jason. I tossed my weapon behind the tree where I knew it would fade from sight.

Tommy jumped out of the first car, never even having seen my friends. He made a beeline to Jason while Officer Clark hustled out of the second car and collected the gun. I watched Tommy put handcuffs around Jason's wrists, taking a deep breath and exhaling slowly to release the tension that had built up inside me.

"Are you okay?" he asked me as he helped his prisoner to his feet. I nodded.

"How did you know I was here?"

"I looked into that tip you gave me about Walter having a grandson," Tommy said. "Turns out he does, but it isn't Larry Greenwood. His name is Jacob Riley," he nodded towards Jason. "I put two and two together when I checked out the grandson's driver's license photo.

We were already on our way to bring him in for questioning when we heard the gunshot."

That certainly explained why I couldn't hold *Dominion* over him. As I had guessed, Jason Briggs wasn't his real name.

"Look at her! Can't you see she's not human?" Jason spat. "Look at her skin and her eyes! My god, she has elf ears!"

I cringed and peeked over at Tommy, worried how he would react to Jason's outburst. The officer glanced at me and smiled.

"She looks like a tattooed teenager to me," he said with a wink in my direction.

CHAPTER 26

"*H*ere, drink this. It will warm you and soothe your voice," Michan said, handing me a mug of steaming liquid.

"What is it?" I sniffed it warily.

"Ginger tea with a touch of lemon. I got lucky and found some in the kitchen. Go ahead now, drink it up." The Brounie waited with a stern expression until I took a sip. It tasted great and it thawed my chilled insides, but he didn't need to know that.

"Have you met Ida Kraus? She's always telling me what I should and shouldn't eat. You two would make a good pair," I said, grabbing a couple of fries from the plate in front of me.

"Thank goodness we're around to take care of you," Cormac interjected. "We must watch over you more closely from now on." I groaned, imagining what life would be like under heavy surveillance. Cormac tutted at my reaction. "Well, you obviously don't know how to take care of yourself. If Aisling hadn't sensed the change in your consciousness, we never would have known to go outside to listen to the wind."

"At least I was smart enough to put words on the wind in the first place," I said, narrowing my eyes at him. There was one thing that had been bothering me ever since the whole debacle with Jason had concluded. "Speaking of taking care of people, how could you let Padraig drop into a gun fight?"

"That child defied my order to stay at the shop with Max," he informed me. He shook his head in disgust. "I told him to go up one of the trees and hide there when I realized he'd followed us, which he couldn't seem to manage either. As a consequence, he's learning the human concept of a babysitter as we speak."

Aisling stuck her head through the door. "Guys, we're up. They're calling for us," she said, beckoning for us to follow her.

My heart sank as we stepped into the restaurant's dining room. Far from the empty audience Cormac had promised, the crowd was standing room only. Ida and her friends sat at a table in the middle of the room. Padraig was sitting with them with a pout on his face, his arms crossed and his dangling feet kicking back and forth.

The firefighters from that afternoon were among a group of men having beers at the bar. Tasha was eating dessert, looking relaxed for once with her husband and children. I spotted a few more friendly faces mixed in among the strangers. The number of Findale residents in the room made things even worse. If I screwed up, it would haunt me forever. It would give them yet another reason to reject me, as they had rejected me so many times in Faery. If the room had been full of strangers, we all could have gone about our merry ways and I'd never see them again.

The chatter in the restaurant settled as we made our way to the stage. Michan's guitar and Aisling's drums waited for them there, along with an electric keyboard. Cormac and I carried instruments on with us. He would alternate between his fiddle and the keyboard depending on the song, just as I would be switching between playing the flute and singing.

"Ladies and gentlemen, thanks for coming out to JR's tonight. We're called *The Gentry*, and we'd like to play a few tunes for your entertainment," Cormac said into the microphone. There was a light splattering of applause as he stepped back and placed his fiddle under his chin.

We opened our set with an old reel written for the fiddle and flute. I had confidence in my flute playing and enjoyed performing the frolicking music, but my anxiety began to rise again as we grew closer to the end of the song. I dreaded what came next.

The audience began clapping to the beat of the peppy tune, encouraging us as the song went along. The rhythmic clapping turned to applause when Cormac drew his bow across his strings to play the final note.

We moved right into our next selection: my first performance singing to a real audience. I stepped up to the microphone, running everything Cormac had taught me through my mind, hoping the lessons had stuck. Cormac placed his fiddle on its stand and moved over to the keyboard. I glanced over at him as he played the song's introduction, wondering how I had let him talk me into this. He gave me an encouraging smile.

I looked out at the audience and tried to forget them. I concentrated on the song instead. The lyrics told the story of a young woman longing for her sweetheart who had traveled across the sea. I felt her love and her pain as the words flowed out of me. As I tenderly sang the last note of the ballad, my heart ached as if I had actually lived through the experience.

There was a moment of silence, broken only by Aisling sniffling behind me. I held my breath, not sure how well I had performed. All at once the crowd jumped to their feet, whooping and cheering for us as they applauded.

Taken aback, I didn't know how to react at first. I glanced over at Cormac, looking for guidance. "I told you so," he mouthed to me with a smile.

The audience kept clapping until I finally took a little bow. Perhaps I was more like a typical Sidhe than I realized. I think I could learn to love performing.

*If you enjoyed this book please take a moment to leave a
short review on the page where you bought the book.*
Reviews are very important to authors because they help
other readers find the book. Your help with this is
sincerely appreciated.

THANK YOU!

Sign up to be on the author's VIP List and Get This Short Story FREE!

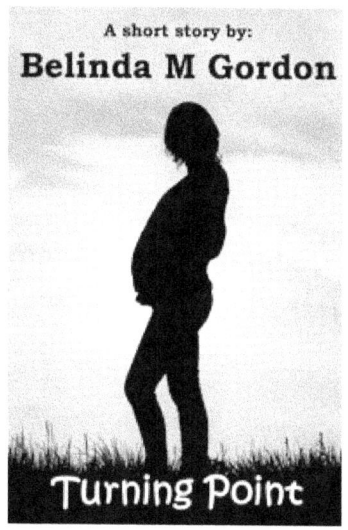

Holly has vowed never to lay eyes on her abusive husband again. When he comes up on trial for murder, both sides pressure her to testify for them. Holly must choose between keeping her vow or succumbing to her family's wishes.

Set in the world of *The King's Jewel Series*, between *Tressa's Treasures* and *Xander's Folly*

Click HERE or go to
www.belinda-gordon.com/newsletter/

ABOUT THE AUTHOR

 Belinda M Gordon was born and raised in Pennsylvania and currently lives in Northeastern PA with her wonderfully supportive husband, her dog, Kip. She is of Irish heritage, which is how she became interested in Celtic Mythology. She used the Celtic Mythology, specifically of Ireland, as the starting point of her Romance/Fantasy series, The King's Jewel and her new series The Finale Far Mysteries.

To learn more about Belinda visit her website at
www.belinda-gordon.com